D0553562

CANDIDE

VOLTAIRE

CANDIDE

or, Optimism

Translated by Peter Constantine

MODERN LIBRARY

NEW YORK

2005 Modern Library Edition

 Published in the United States by Modern Library, an imprint of The Random House Publishing Group, a division of Random House, Inc., New York, and simultaneously in Canada by Random House of Canada Limited, Toronto.

LIBRARY OF CONGRESS CATALOGING-IN-PUBLICATION DATA
Voltaire, 1694–1778.
[Candide. English]
Candide, or, optimism / by Voltaire ; translated by Peter Constantine.
p. cm.
ISBN 0-679-64313-3
I. Title: Candide. II. Title: Optimism.
III. Constantine, Peter, 1963– . IV. Title.
PQ2082.C3E5 2005
843'.5—dc22 2004055244

Modern Library website address: www.modernlibrary.com

Printed in the United States of America on acid-free paper

2 4 6 8 9 7 5 3

VOLTAIRE

Voltaire was one of the greatest French writers and philosophers—the embodiment of eighteenth-century Enlightenment, which has been called *le siècle de Voltaire,* the century of Voltaire. His writing sparkles with wit and criticism, and was instrumental in spreading ideas of reason and tolerance. He was one of the most forceful and effective crusaders against tyranny and bigotry.

Voltaire's life was stormy from the start. His birth certificate states that he was born in Paris on November 21, 1694, though he often claimed that his birth had been kept secret for some nine months and his actual date of birth was February 20 of that year. He was born François-Marie Arouet, but coined the pen name Voltaire when he was twenty-three, after he had been imprisoned in the Bastille for almost a year for implying in a satirical poem that the prince regent had had an incestuous liaison with his daughter.

From his earliest years, Voltaire had a hostile relationship with his father, a notary who managed to secure for himself the position of receiver in the Cour des Comptes, the Court of Accounts, which had jurisdiction over the financial affairs of the French public sector. Voltaire later claimed that he was actually the son of one Rochebrune, who he said was a "musketeer, officer, author." After his mother's death when he was seven, Voltaire grew closer to his godfather, the Abbé de Châteauneuf, a freethinker and a man of taste who took him along to fashionable literary salons, where the boy was admired for his precocious gift for poetry. The abbé even brought young Voltaire to the salon of his former mistress, the celebrated courtesan Ninon de Lenclos (she was then in her mid-eighties), who was so impressed by the boy that in her will she left him a thousand francs to buy books. "The boy had written a few poems that were worthless, but seemed rather good for his age," she wrote.

When he was ten, Voltaire entered the Jesuit Collège Louis-le-Grand in Paris, one of the best schools in France, whose alumni have included Molière, Diderot, the Marquis de Sade, Hugo, and Baudelaire. He received a solid education in the classics, mathematics, history, and religion, and also made some influential friends among his aristocratic schoolmates, who were to prove useful to Voltaire later in life.

Voltaire's father forced him to study law and, at nineteen, to take on a position as a private secretary to the French ambassador at the Hague. Voltaire was dismissed from the post in disgrace after a romantic entanglement with Olympe ("Pimpette") Dunoyer, whose mother ran a local scandal sheet. Voltaire's father was so furious that he temporarily disinherited him and threatened to have him deported to America.

Back in Paris, Voltaire became a literary man-about-town, much admired for his poetry and wit. His first youthful ventures on the literary scene, however, also ended in scandal when he was exiled to Sully-sur-Loire for seven months for writing a satiric poem questioning the morals of the prince regent's daughter. The following year, another poem—this one questioning the morals of both the regent and the regent's daughter—resulted in his first imprisonment in the Bastille, where he spent almost a year reading Homer in Latin and Greek and writing ("on linen chewed into paper"). There he also began working on his epic poem *La Henriade* and completed his first tragedy, *Oedipe.* Voltaire was released from the Bastille in April 1718, and in November of that year *Oedipe* premiered with resounding success at the Comédie-Française. Young Voltaire was feted as France's new Racine.

Voltaire now frequented the most elegant salons and châteaus, where his sparkling wit and conversation made him a sought-after guest. There he met the foremost writers and thinkers of the day and began making a name for himself as a "philosophe." When *La Henriade* was published to great acclaim in its first version, *La Ligue, ou, Henri le Grand,* Voltaire received a pension of a thousand francs from the same regent who had had him thrown into the Bastille five years earlier, and his career as court poet began. He presented *La tragédie de Mariamne* and the comedy *L'Indiscret* at the marriage celebration of Louis XV. The royal couple was very impressed and awarded him an additional pension of fifteen hundred francs.

At the height of his popularity, another disastrous scandal struck. The Chevalier de Rohan-Chabot, a member of one of the most powerful families in France, exchanged acerbic witticisms with Voltaire about their respective names, the result of which was that Voltaire was beaten up and thrown into the Bastille again, from which he left for England, where he remained in exile for two and a half years.

England had a profound effect on Voltaire. He perfected his English, and met the foremost writers and philosophers of the day: Alexander Pope, Jonathan Swift, William Congreve, George Berkeley, and Samuel Clarke. He was fascinated by the freedom in England, its tolerant society, and its aristocracy, whose social and political influence was limited in comparison to France.

He returned to France in 1729, invigorated and with many manuscripts. He mounted a series of plays influenced by Shakespeare—*Brutus, Eriphile, Les Originaux, La Mort de César*—and *Zaïre,* which was a resounding success. He also mounted the operas *Samson* and *Tanis et Zélide,* and published his first historical work, *Histoire de Charles XII.*

The most important work resulting from his stay in England is the *Lettres philosophiques,* which came out in France in 1734 and created another scandal and another warrant for Voltaire's arrest. The *Lettres* are in the form of a series of fictitious epistles from England, demonstrating the positive effects of religious tolerance and the superiority of English philosophy, art, and science. To escape a third stay in the Bastille, Voltaire again fled Paris. For the next decade, he resided with his mistress Gabrielle-Émilie du Châtelet in her château in Cirey in Champagne, near the border (so he could leave the country in a hurry if he had to). She was one of the foremost intellects of her time and furthered Voltaire's interest in the natural sciences and philosophy.

Voltaire had been in correspondence with Frederick the Great, and when the War of Austrian Succession broke out in 1740, Voltaire undertook missions to rally Frederick's support of the French cause. His success restored him to favor with Louis XV, and he was appointed court biographer and *gentilhomme de la chambre* to the French king. This period of favor, however, ended once more in scandal, in 1747, at the card table of the queen. Voltaire's mistress Madame du Châtelet was losing, and Voltaire rashly warned her in English that the noble ladies at the table were "card-sharpers." Madame du Châtelet noticed the stunned expressions, and the couple fled to Lunéville, to the château of former king Stanislas of Poland. It was during this period that Voltaire began writing his first *contes philosophiques,* his philosophical stories: *Zadig* (1747), *Vision de Babouc* (1748), *Memnon* (1749), and *Micromégas* (1752).

After Madame du Châtelet's death in 1749, Voltaire left France for the court of Frederick the Great. Things began well there, as Voltaire, "the King of Philosophers," consorted with Frederick, "the Philosopher King." Voltaire was heaped with honors and medals, given a handsome pension, and his plays were performed and applauded. But neither the king nor Voltaire could refrain from caustic witticisms. Scandals soon followed. Voltaire filed a lawsuit against a moneylender and argued with Frederick's courtiers. When Voltaire ridiculed the president of the Berlin Academy in his pamphlet *Diatribe du docteur Akakia,* Frederick was outraged, had the public hangman burn all the pamphlets, and Voltaire fled Prussia for France. Louis XV, however, forbade him to return to Paris, and Voltaire settled in Geneva.

There, too, Voltaire was at first welcomed and showered with honors, but he soon clashed with the local Calvinists and literary figures. A major scandal erupted when Diderot and d'Alembert's *Encyclopédie* was published. Voltaire had supplied information for the entry on Geneva, which many of its citizens felt was defamatory. He left Geneva for the Castle of Schwetzingen, in Württemberg, where he wrote his most famous work, *Candide, ou, l'optimisme* (1759).

Voltaire subsequently settled on an estate at Ferney in

France, on the Swiss border, where he could escape to Switzerland, or then back to France, as the need arose. One of the most active periods of his life ensued: He ran his estate with great efficiency along new agricultural principles, built factories on his land to provide employment for local villagers, entertained a glittering array of aristocrats and literary figures, and cultivated a vast and energetic correspondence with actors, philosophers, politicians, princes, and kings. He edited the works of Corneille, wrote commentaries on Racine, and published the *Dictionnaire philosophique portatif* (1764)—the first portable work of its kind—and wrote his famous works *L'Ingenu* (1767), *La Princesse de Babylone* (1768), and *Le Taureau blanc* (1774).

Voltaire, now a world-famous figure, used his influence and authority to battle injustice and religious and political persecution, which he did with vigor and remarkable success. But he also went to extremes in attacking rivals and former colleagues and friends whom he suspected of conspiring against him.

After many years of exile from Paris, Voltaire returned in 1778 to direct the rehearsals of his play *Irène.* The fanfare triggered by his return to Paris was astonishing. He was swamped by friends and admirers, feted, paraded to the Académie Française, and at the premiere of *Irène* was crowned in his box. The excitement was too much, however, and he died on May 30, at the age of eighty-three. Before an ecclesiastic prohibition for a Christian burial could be served, Voltaire's nephew, the Abbé Mignot, had his body transported to the chapel of the Abbey of Scellières. There Voltaire was given a quick and discreet Christian burial. His remains were transferred to the Panthéon in Paris during the French Revolution.

INTRODUCTION

Diane Johnson

Candide is, for the English reader, Voltaire's most familiar work, a production of his maturity—written when he was sixty-five—and seems to present in most concise and apposite form the considered opinions of his life. In this odd work, a credulous young hero, Candide, is driven, like Adam from Eden, out of the happy precincts of his childhood in Westphalia, which in Voltaire's day was in reality one of the poorest and most embattled parts of Germany. *Candide* is set in this distant German province at least in part to protect the author from any supposition that it was intended to comment on the political situation or moral condition of France. Voltaire had had a number of run-ins with kings and cardinals because of his volatile political writings, and was pointedly careful to avoid direct references to recognizable autocrats. Indeed, like many of his colleagues and friends, he had been imprisoned a number of times in the Bastille, imprisonments, to be sure, made comfortable enough by the rules of the day—but prison all the same. Though wishing to avoid its consequences, he throve on political controversy and courted it constantly. *Candide* was only one of his Swiftean attacks on political abuses, but it is somehow the one that has remained current.

Without reference to the real events of Voltaire's time, and to the ideas he contributed with his satire to the evolving social and political discourse, *Candide* can seem a picaresque tale of limited fascination. One soon understands the design: a naïve young man, trustfully adhering to the lessons of his fatuous teacher, Professor Pangloss, that all is created for the best in this best of all possible worlds, is launched into a series of adventures that reasonably would lead most people to despair. His intended wife, Cunégonde, is kidnapped, raped, and eviscerated. He himself is kidnapped, beaten, imprisoned, loses his home, and loses his loved one.

Though the characters miraculously survive most of the horrors they suffer—for basically Voltaire is an optimist—the contrast between what they suffer and their optimism serves only to point up the folly of belief in general and optimism in particular. Everyone Candide encounters exemplifies the greed and brutality that seem to characterize mankind, though he himself, Cunégonde, Pangloss, and their other companions are finally the very models of people who survive by patiently focusing on their work. This was Voltaire's own recipe for survival, and there may be more than a bit of himself as he thought of himself in the naïve, good, and good-looking Candide.

The hundreds of books that have been written about Voltaire, the most admired and famous writer of the eighteenth century and perhaps for us the most famous of all French writers, together give the vivid impression of an amazing human being—merry, difficult, brilliant, indefatigable, productive, witty, and wise. It may be helpful to an American reader to place him in his epoch, complete with powdered wig and ruffled neckcloth, by remembering that

Voltaire and Benjamin Franklin knew each other and shared the paradoxically hopeful cynicism that seems to characterize the late eighteenth century.

They were introduced in Paris by admirers who believed that these two great thinkers should meet. Whether either had ever heard of the other is unclear, but at the urging of a crowd at a meeting of the scientific society, they politely embraced and perhaps exchanged a few words—in which language is not recorded, but it was likely English, for Voltaire knew English well, read it, and had even written in English; he had spent a few years in exile in England during one of his many periods of being in disfavor with two of the three kings Louis who reigned during his long lifetime. This disfavor was earned by his lifelong, vigilant criticism of a variety of the political and humanitarian issues pungently expressed in *Candide*.

Above all was Voltaire's belief in freedom. At the time of his meeting with Franklin in 1778, the American Revolution was in full force, and Voltaire was predicting a French one that he would not live to see. He died the same year, at the age of eighty-four, in the reign of Louis XVI, praising the revolution that must inevitably come.

> I won't have the pleasure of beholding it. The French catch on to everything late, but they understand at last. Young people are lucky—they will see great things. I shall not cease to preach tolerance upon the housetops until persecution is no more. The progress of right is slow. The roots of prejudice are deep. I shall never see the fruits of my efforts, but their seeds must one day germinate.

Later thinkers would agree that his ideas on individuality, industry, religion, and human rights may have indeed fostered the French Revolution, which followed the

American one by thirteen years, and must also have influenced the earlier one, given that Jefferson, Franklin, and indeed Washington, all valued his works. (Though Jefferson never met Voltaire, he kept a copy of Houdon's bust of him at Monticello.)

"Voltaire" was a nom de plume he invented after the success of his first literary works; he was born François-Marie Arouet in November (or February) 1694, in the reign of Louis XIV. The particle he gave himself (in "Arouet de Voltaire") suggests a certain conflict about his own place in society. Though his father was a member of the bourgeoisie, a prosperous *notaire* (a kind of legal functionary), the boy had the common (according to Freud) fantasy of being of noble birth, and thought of himself as the illegitimate son of an aristocratic neighbor. Whatever his parentage, he was exceptional, and excelled at his studies, though the ideas of the Jesuits who taught him only incited his mockery and anticlericalism. Like Jefferson and Franklin, he counted himself a Deist and was a lifelong resolute critic of the Catholic church and of religion in general. Religious skepticism among freethinking French intellectuals (again like the American founders) had generally replaced unquestioning, conventional piety, and neither Deism nor atheism was actively persecuted. Yet *Candide,* when it was published in 1759, would be condemned in both Catholic France and Protestant Geneva.

The temperament that initially led young Arouet to study law accounts for his interest in politics and even his role as a French spy, when adviser to his friend Frederick the Great of Prussia, and for his bitter portrayal of rulers in *Candide.* Though he became very rich, like other artists and intellectuals of the period, he had a lively sense of the prevailing idea of noblesse oblige, and he had a number of patrons, of whom Frederick was the most highly placed. He never married, but lived for twenty years with the great love of his life, the almost equally remarkable Madame du Châtelet, a young, rich, and intellectually ambitious aristocrat, in a chateau tactfully distant from the court, where they did scientific experiments and entertained a variety of courtiers, intellectuals, and the simply amusing among their friends. When Madame du Châtelet died (after giving birth to a child by another lover), Voltaire lived with King Frederick, still later with his niece (said also to be his mistress) and, until his last year, at his own estate on the Swiss border at Ferney, where he could escape France when, as often happened, his outspoken criticisms of the crown endangered his freedom. He had just moved to Ferney while he was writing *Candide,* and was greatly under the charm of rural domestic life, as we see from the tale's denouement.

The almost casual brutalities—torture, mutilation, rape, and murder—that the hapless Candide and his beloved Cunégonde behold or endure in their flight from Westphalia are perhaps shocking to the modern reader, yet they are only slight exaggerations of actual practices in Voltaire's world. To be sure, France in the seventeenth century, which produced Voltaire himself at the end of it, had slightly improved over its northern neighbors. The bitter wars of religion that had raged during the sixteenth and seventeenth centuries and had divided all of Europe, and within France pitted Catholics against Huguenots, had somewhat subsided but were still very much in Voltaire's mind.

In the middle of their travels and misfortunes, Candide and his party at one period find themselves in El Dorado, a marvelous, peaceable land, more or less Peru, full of gold and jewels that people are not driven to acquire, wonderful food, religious tolerance, an enlightened king, and general happiness. This astonishing place makes Candide and his company almost uncomfortable, and too excited by the prospect of going back home laden with jewels and gold to remain. They resume their journeys, having to spend all their fortune on bribing and hiring their way back to Europe to rescue Cunégonde.

When eventually Candide and his companions are able to find and save her, she has become hideously ugly. He marries her anyway, still trusting that everything is for the best in this best of all possible worlds, the credo, intended as a satire on Leibnitz, that Dr. Pangloss has not wavered from. They settle down on a small farm, where each exercises his talents, far from "boredom, vice, and want," and endorses the principal that each of us must "cultivate his garden."

Despite its specific targets, in *Candide,* it is the entire human race—greedy, cruel, inconstant—that is called into question:

> "Do you believe that men always butchered one another the way they do today?" Candide asked. "Do you believe they have always been liars, rogues, traitors, ingrates, brigands, weaklings, inconstant, cowards, enviers, gluttons, drunkards, misers, self-seekers, bloodthirsty, slanderers, debauchees, fanatics, hypocrites, and fools?"
>
> "Do you believe that hawks have always eaten pigeons wherever they have found them?" Martin asked.

By the time he wrote this, Voltaire had seen enough of humanity and its institutions to confirm his harsh opinion of them. Perhaps current events have given contemporary Americans more of a sense of the effects of religious fanaticism than we could have had even a few decades ago.

Roland Barthes remarked in 1964, of the pertinence of Voltaire's philosophy, that while today we have no Inquisition, ours is still a world rife with persecutions and horrors committed in religion's name. He believed that only the theater, the spectacle of persecution, had vanished, and the bonfire and axe supplanted by more insidious methods of torture and killing. But at the beginning of the third millennium we are in a position to say that the theater has been rediscovered, too, with video-taped beheadings—and Voltaire's dim view of human nature is confirmed.

Yet, is his an entirely dim view? The complex mixture of cynicism and optimism in *Candide,* which is subtitled *ou, l'optimisme,* has generated numerous arguments. Is it finally Voltaire's view that man is redeemed, and his life made worth living, by the exercise of hope, good nature, and industry (*"cultiver son jardin"*) in the face of cruelty and wickedness? Or is this simply the warring of his own good nature with the plain facts apparent to his intelligence, of the fundamental cruel and wicked character of mankind? The reader can make this judgment for himself.

—

DIANE JOHNSON is the author of ten novels, most recently *Le Mariage* and *Le Divorce,* two books of essays, two biographies, and the screenplay for Stanley Kubrick's classic film *The Shining.* She has been a finalist four times for the Pulitzer Prize and the National Book Award.

CANDIDE

*or, Optimism**

Translated from the German of Dr. Ralph,
with addenda found in the doctor's pocket
when he died at Minden
in the year of grace
1759

* *Optimism* was a neologism at the time. It refers to the philosophical doctrine that events are organized in view of the good of man, and that the world is the best of all possible worlds.

Chapter One

How Candide was raised in a fine castle, and how he was chased from it

In Westphalia, in the castle of Baron Thunder-Ten-Tronckh, there lived a young boy whom nature had endowed with the sweetest disposition. His face was a reflection of his soul. His judgment was fairly straightforward and his mind of the simplest. It is for this reason, I believe, that he was named Candide. The old servants of the castle suspected that he was the son of the baron's sister and a good and honest gentleman of those parts whom the young lady did not wish to marry, as he could claim only seventy-one heraldic quarterings of noble lineage, the rest of his family tree having been lost to the ravages of time.*

The baron was one of the most powerful lords of Westphalia, for his castle had windows and a door. His great hall was even adorned with a tapestry. All the dogs from his farmyards were rounded up into a hunting pack whenever the need arose, and his grooms acted as his hunting whips. The vicar of the village served as his private almoner. Everyone called the baron "Your Grace" and laughed at his stories.

* Heraldic quarterings are the noble arms of other families that an individual acquires in his or her coat of arms through marriages. Voltaire is satirizing the German nobility's pride in its lineages: seventy-one quarterings of noble lineage is extraordinarily high.

The baroness, whose weight of some three hundred and fifty pounds had made her a figure of considerable importance, carried out the honors of the household with a dignity that made her even more respectable. Her daughter, Cunégonde, seventeen years of age, had a flushed complexion and was fresh, fat, and piquant. The baron's son seemed in every respect worthy of his father. Pangloss, the tutor, was the oracle of the house, and young Candide followed his lessons with all the good faith of his age and character.*

Pangloss taught metaphysico-theologo-cosmo-idiotology. He could demonstrate quite admirably that there is no effect without a cause, and that in this best of all possible worlds, His Grace the Baron's castle was the finest of castles and Her Grace the Baroness the best of all possible baronesses.

"It has been demonstrated," Pangloss used to say, "that things cannot be otherwise: for as everything has been made for a purpose, everything is necessarily made for the best purpose. Note that noses were made to bear spectacles, and hence we have spectacles. Legs were obviously instituted in order to wear breeches, and hence we have breeches. Stones were formed to be quarried and used to build castles, and hence His Grace has a very fine castle. The greatest baron of the province must also be the best housed. And as pigs have been made to be eaten, we eat pork all year round. Consequently, those who propose that all is well are talking nonsense: They should say that all is best."†

* The word *pangloss* is Greek for "all language."

† Voltaire is satirizing the doctrines of the German philosopher and mathematician Leibniz, 1646–1716, who argued that God created the best of all possible worlds. Throughout *Candide*, Voltaire also satirizes Leibniz's view that nothing happens without sufficient reason.

Candide listened attentively and believed innocently, for he found Mademoiselle Cunégonde extremely beautiful, even if he had never summoned up the courage to tell her so. He concluded that after the good fortune of being born Baron Thunder-Ten-Tronckh, the second degree of good fortune was to be Mademoiselle Cunégonde, the third to see her every day, and the fourth to hear Doctor Pangloss, the greatest philosopher in all the province and, consequently, the world.

One day Cunégonde was walking near the castle in a small wood that was called "the park," when she saw Doctor Pangloss in the underbrush giving a lesson in experimental physics to her mother's chambermaid, a pretty and obedient brunette. As Mademoiselle Cunégonde had a great aptitude for science, she watched with bated breath the repeated experiments to which she was witness. She perceived with great clarity the doctor's sufficient reason, the effects and their causes, and returned to the castle quite excited, deep in thought, and filled with the desire to be learned, reflecting that she could well be young Candide's sufficient reason, and that he could also be hers.

As she was returning to the castle, she happened upon Candide and blushed. Candide blushed too. She greeted him in a faltering voice, and Candide spoke to her without knowing what he was saying. The following day, after dinner, as everyone left the table, Cunégonde and Candide encountered each other behind a screen. Cunégonde dropped her handkerchief, Candide picked it up, she innocently took his hand, and the young man innocently kissed hers with exceptional vivacity, feeling, and grace. Their lips met, their eyes flashed, their knees trembled, and their hands strayed. Baron Thunder-Ten-Tronckh walked past the screen and, observing this cause and effect, chased

Candide from the castle with hard kicks to his backside. Cunégonde fainted, and the baroness slapped her the instant she came to. And all was consternation in this finest and most charming of all possible castles.

Chapter Two

*What happened to Candide among the Bulgars**

Chased from the terrestrial paradise, Candide wandered for a long time without knowing where he was going, weeping, raising his eyes to Heaven, but turning them more often back to the most beautiful of castles, which contained the most beautiful of young baronesses. He lay down to sleep without dinner between two furrows in a field. Snow fell in large flakes. Candide, frozen through, dragged himself, penniless and dying of hunger and exhaustion, to the neighboring town of Valdberghoff-Trarbk-Dikdorff. He stopped with heavy heart outside a tavern door. Two men dressed in blue noticed him.

"Comrade," one said to the other. "Here is a well-built young man of the required height."

They approached Candide and very civilly asked him to dine with them.

"You do me great honor, gentlemen," Candide replied with charming modesty. "But I have no money with which to pay my share."

"Ah, sir," one of the men in blue replied. "A man of your build and merit need not pay a thing. Aren't you five feet five inches tall?"

* The name Bulgars is a jibing reference to the Prussian troops under Frederick the Great, 1712–1786. From the medieval Latin *bulgarus,* meaning *heretic,* or *sodomite.*

"Yes, gentlemen, that is my height," Candide replied with a bow.

"Ah, sir, sit down at the table. Not only will we pay for your meal, but we cannot abide that a man like you lacks money. Men were made to help one another."

"You are right," Candide said. "That is what Doctor Pangloss always told me, and I can see that everything is for the best."

They begged him to accept a few coins. He took them and started to write out a promissory note, but they adamantly refused, and they all sat down to dinner.

"Are you devoted to—?"

"Oh, yes!" Candide immediately replied. "I am devoted to Mademoiselle Cunégonde."

"No, we meant are you devoted to the King of the Bulgars?" one of the gentlemen said.

"Not in the least. I have never laid eyes on him," Candide replied.

"How can that be? He is the most charming of kings, we must drink to his health!"

"Oh, gladly, gentlemen!" And he drank.

"That's enough," they said. "You are now the support, the prop, the defender, the hero of the Bulgars. Your fortune is made and your glory assured."

Candide's feet were immediately put in irons, and he was taken to the regiment. He was ordered to right face, left face, present arms, order arms, take aim, fire, double his pace, and was given thirty strokes of the rod. The following day he did the exercise a little less badly and got only twenty strokes; the day after only ten, and was viewed by his comrades as a prodigy.

Candide was astounded. He could not yet understand what made him a hero. One fine spring day he took it into his head to go off, walking straight ahead, believing it to be the privilege of mankind, as of animals, to make use of their legs at will. He had not gone two leagues when four other heroes, six feet tall, caught up with him, tied him up, and threw him into a dungeon. He was asked by the court-martial if he preferred being flogged thirty-six times by the entire regiment or having twelve bullets shot into his brain all at once. There was no point in his arguing that man's will is free, and that he wanted neither the one punishment nor the other: he had to choose. He decided, by virtue of the divine gift known as freedom of choice, to run the gauntlet thirty-six times. He endured two runs. The regiment was composed of two thousand men. That came to four thousand strokes of the rod, which exposed every muscle and nerve from the nape of his neck to his bottom. As he was about to begin his third run, Candide, unable to take any more, begged them to show mercy and grant him the favor of riddling his brain instead. The favor was granted. He was blindfolded and made to kneel. At that moment the King of the Bulgars passed by and inquired what the culprit's crime had been, and as the king was a man of great genius, he understood from everything he heard about Candide that he was a young metaphysician who was blissfully ignorant of the ways of the world, and pardoned him with a clemency that will be praised in all the newspapers and throughout the ages. A worthy surgeon healed Candide in three weeks with ointments decreed by Dioscorides.* Some of his skin had already grown back, and when the King of the Bulgars declared war on the King of the Avars, Candide could walk again.†

* Pedanius Dioscorides, c. 40–90 C.E., Greek physician and scientist. His five-volume *De materia medica* had been the most influential pharmacological work in Europe until the end of the fifteenth century. Voltaire is implying that the Prussian medical expertise is behind the times.

† Voltaire is referring to the Seven Years' War, 1756–1763. The French are represented by the Avars, a mounted nomad people who dominated Central Asia

Chapter Three

How Candide escaped from among the Bulgars, and what became of him

Nothing was as beautiful, smart, dazzling, or well ordered as the two armies. The trumpets, fifes, oboes, drums, and cannons created a harmony such as never existed in Hell. First of all, the cannons struck down almost six thousand men on each side. Then the muskets removed from the best of worlds between nine and ten thousand rogues infecting its surface. The bayonet was also the sufficient reason for the death of several thousand men. The total might well have come to some thirty thousand souls. Candide, trembling like a philosopher, hid himself as best he could during this heroic butchery.

Finally, while the two kings had the Te Deum sung, each in his camp, Candide decided to go elsewhere to reason over effects and causes. Climbing over heaps of dead and dying men, he arrived at a neighboring village that lay in ashes: it was an Avar village that the Bulgars had burnt down in accordance with the principles of international law. Old men covered in wounds watched their butchered wives die clasping their infants to their bleeding breasts. Girls who had been disemboweled after having sated the natural needs of some of the heroes were breathing their last. Others, covered in burns, were begging to be put out of their misery. Brains were splattered on the ground alongside severed arms and legs.

---

and Eastern Europe from the fourth to the eighth century C.E. Voltaire has Dr. Ralph, who is identified on the title page as the supposed author of *Candide*, die in the Battle of Minden in 1759.

Candide fled as fast as he could to another village. This one belonged to the Bulgars, and the Avar heroes had treated it the same way. Stepping over palpitating limbs and climbing over ruins, Candide, carrying a few provisions in his bag, finally managed to get out of the theater of war, never forgetting Mademoiselle Cunégonde. His provisions ran out when he reached Holland, but having heard that everyone in that country was rich and Christian, he did not doubt that he would be treated as well as he had been at the castle of His Lordship the Baron before he was driven from it on account of Mademoiselle Cunégonde's beautiful eyes.

He asked for alms from several grave personages, all of whom replied that if he continued plying this trade he would be locked up in a house of correction, where he would be taught how to work for a living.

Then he approached a man who had just addressed a big crowd for a whole hour on the topic of charity. The orator eyed him suspiciously and asked, "What are you doing here? Did you come for the Good Cause?"

"There is no effect without a cause," Candide replied modestly. "Everything is necessarily interconnected and arranged for the best. I had to be driven out of the presence of Mademoiselle Cunégonde, run the gauntlet, and beg for bread until I can earn my own. All this could not be otherwise."

"My friend," the orator said, "do you believe that the Pope is the Antichrist?"

"I have never yet heard that he is," Candide replied. "But whether he is the Antichrist or not, I need bread."

"You don't deserve any," the orator said. "Go away, you rogue, you wretch! Don't come near me again as long as you live!"

The orator's wife poked her head out the window and,

seeing the man who doubted that the Pope was the Antichrist, poured out on his head a chamber pot full of . . .

Merciful Heaven! To what excess ladies will carry the zeal of religion!

A man who had not been baptized, a good Anabaptist by the name of Jacques, saw the cruel and disgraceful manner in which one of his brothers, a featherless, two-legged being with a soul, was being treated.* He took him to his place, washed him, gave him bread and beer, made him a gift of two florins, and even wanted to teach him to work in his factory, which manufactured Persian fabrics in Holland. Candide almost prostrated himself before him, exclaiming, "Doctor Pangloss had told me that everything is for the best in this world. I am infinitely more moved by your extreme generosity than by the severity of that man in the black cloak and his wife."

The following day, Candide was out walking when he came across a beggar covered in pustules. He had lifeless eyes, a nose that was rotting away, a mouth that was twisted, black teeth, and a rasping voice. He coughed violently, spitting out a tooth every time.

* The Anabaptists were an extreme Protestant sect that did not believe in infant baptism—in their view only adult baptism was valid. They believed in absolute social and religious equality. "A featherless, two-legged being" is a humorous reference to Plato's definition of man.

Chapter Four

How Candide met his old philosophy tutor Doctor Pangloss, and what followed

Candide, touched more by compassion than by horror, gave the repugnant beggar the two florins he had been given by his good Anabaptist friend Jacques. The phantom stared at him, burst into tears, and flung himself around his neck. Candide recoiled.

"Alas!" said one wretch to the other. "Do you not recognize your dear Pangloss?"

"What do I hear? Is that you, my dear master, you, in this terrible condition? What misfortune has befallen you? Why are you no longer in the finest of all castles? What has become of Mademoiselle Cunégonde, that pearl among women, that masterpiece of nature?"

"I am at the end of my strength," Pangloss said.

Candide immediately led him to the Anabaptist's stable, where he gave him a little bread to eat. When Pangloss had recovered, Candide asked him again, "Well, what has become of Cunégonde?"

"She's dead," the other replied.

Candide fainted at the word. His friend revived him with some bad vinegar he happened to find in the stable. Candide opened his eyes. "Cunégonde dead? O best of all worlds, where are you? But what illness did she die of? Surely not from having seen me driven out from the fine castle by His Lordship her father with kicks to the backside?"

"No," Pangloss replied, "she was disemboweled by Bulgar soldiers, after she was raped as much as one can be. His

Lordship tried to defend her, but they bashed his head in, and Her Ladyship the Baroness was hacked to pieces. As for my poor pupil, he met the same fate as his sister. And as for the castle, not a stone was left standing, not a barn, not a sheep, not a duck, not a tree. But we were well avenged, for the Avars did exactly the same to a neighboring barony belonging to a Bulgar lord."

At this account Candide fainted again. But regaining his senses, and having said everything he had to say, he asked about the cause and effect, and the sufficient reason that had reduced Pangloss to such a pitiful state.

"Alas, it was love," Pangloss replied. "Love, the consoler of mankind, the preserver of the universe, the soul of all sensitive beings, tender love."

"Alas," Candide said, "I have known that love, the sovereign of hearts, the soul of our soul. It never brought me more than a kiss and twenty kicks to the backside. How could this fine cause produce in you such an abominable effect?"

Pangloss replied as follows: "Oh, my dear Candide! You knew Paquette, our august baroness's pretty maid. In her arms I tasted the delights of Paradise, which produced these torments of Hell you see devouring me. She was infected by the disease, and has perhaps died of it. She had received the gift from a very learned Franciscan, who took pains to trace the disease back to its source. He was given it by an old countess, who had it from a cavalry captain, who owed it to a marquise, who got it from a page, who had received it from a Jesuit, who as a novice had it in direct line from one of Christopher Columbus's companions. As for me, I will not give it to anyone, for I am dying."

"O Pangloss, what a strange genealogy!" Candide exclaimed. "Isn't the Devil at the root of it?"

"Not at all," the great man replied. "It was an indispensable thing in the best of all possible worlds, a necessary ingredient. For if Columbus on an island of the Americas had not caught this illness that poisons the source of generation, often even hindering generation, a disease that is evidently the opposite of the grand purpose of nature, we would have neither chocolate nor cochineal. I must also point out that until today this illness, like controversy, has been limited to our continent. Turks, Indians, Persians, Chinese, Siamese, and the Japanese do not know it yet. But there is sufficient reason for them to become acquainted with it in their turn over the next few centuries. In the meantime, it has made astonishing progress among us, above all among the great armies of honest, well-brought-up mercenaries who decide the destiny of nations. One can be certain that when thirty thousand men fight in a battle, ranged against the same number of troops, there are on each side about twenty thousand men with the pox."

"How admirable," Candide said. "But you have to be cured!"

"How can I be?" Pangloss replied. "I don't have a sou to my name, my friend, and in the whole expanse of our globe you will neither be bled nor given an enema without paying, or without someone paying for you."

This last statement decided Candide. He went to throw himself at the feet of his charitable Anabaptist friend Jacques and painted such a touching picture of the state to which Doctor Pangloss had been reduced that the good man did not hesitate to take him in. He had him cured at his expense, and during the treatment Pangloss lost only an eye and an ear. Pangloss could write nicely and was well versed in arithmetic. Jacques the Anabaptist made him his bookkeeper. At the end of two months, having to go to Lisbon on business, he took the two philosophers with him on the boat. Pangloss explained to him how everything could not be better, but Jacques was not of that opinion.

"Men must have had a corrupting effect on nature," the Anabaptist said, "for though they are not born wolves, they have become wolves. God has given them neither twenty-four-pounder cannons nor bayonets, and yet they have made bayonets and cannons to destroy each other. I could also cite the bankrupts, and the law that seizes their goods in order to deprive the creditors of their money."

"All of that was necessary," the one-eyed doctor replied. "Individual misfortunes result in the general good, with the consequence that the more individual misfortune there is, the more everything is for the best."

While he was reasoning thus the sky darkened, the winds blew from the four corners of the earth, and the ship, already within sight of the port of Lisbon, was assailed by the most terrible storm.

Chapter Five

Storm, shipwreck, earthquake, and what became of Doctor Pangloss, Candide, and Jacques the Anabaptist

Half the passengers, weakened and dying of the unimaginable agonies the rolling of a ship can cause to all the nerves and humors of the body when these are shaken in opposite directions, did not even have the strength to worry about the danger. The other half were shrieking and praying. The sails were in tatters, the masts broken, the hull splitting. Whoever could pitched in, but as there was no one in charge, no one knew what to do. The Anabaptist, standing on the upper deck, was trying to help steer the vessel when a frenzied sailor punched him with such force that he was laid out on the deck. The sailor himself was jolted so violently from the blow he had delivered that he fell overboard headfirst and hung suspended from a broken piece of mast. Good Jacques rushed to the sailor's rescue and helped him climb back onboard but fell into the sea from the effort, the sailor letting him perish without so much as a glance. Candide saw his benefactor reappear on the surface for a moment, only to be swallowed by the waves forever. Candide wanted to jump in after him, but the philosopher Pangloss prevented him, demonstrating that the harbor of Lisbon had been purposely created for the Anabaptist to drown in. While he was demonstrating this a priori, the ship broke up and everyone perished except for Pangloss, Candide, and the brute of a sailor who had brought about the drowning of the virtuous Anabaptist. The rogue blithely swam to shore, while Pangloss and Candide were borne there on a plank.

When they had recovered a little, they made their way to Lisbon. They still had a few coins, with which they hoped to save themselves from starvation now that they had escaped the storm.

Still weeping over the death of their benefactor, Candide and Pangloss had hardly set foot in the town when they suddenly felt the earth shaking beneath their feet. The sea seethed in the port, wrecking the ships anchored there, and whirls of fire and ash covered the streets and squares. Houses collapsed, roofs caving in on crumbling foundations. Thirty thousand inhabitants of all ages, both men and women, were crushed beneath the ruins.*

* A catastrophic earthquake destroyed Lisbon on All Saints' Day in 1755. It had a profound effect on European intellectuals, who questioned whether

"There'll be something to be gained here," the sailor said, whistling and swearing.

"What can the sufficient reason for this phenomenon be?" Pangloss asked.

"This is the end of the world!" Candide exclaimed.

The sailor ran blindly into the ruins, facing death to find money, found some, snatched it up, drank himself into a stupor, and after sleeping it off bought the favors of the first girl of goodwill he encountered among the dead and dying in the rubble of the destroyed houses. All the while, Pangloss was pulling the sailor by the sleeve. "My friend," he said to him, "this is not good. You are lacking in universal reason. You are not putting your time to good use."

"God's blood!" the rogue replied. "I am a sailor born in Batavia! On four journeys to Japan I have trampled on the crucifix.* You've found the right person to talk to about your universal reason!"

Candide had been injured by some falling pieces of stone and was lying in the street, wounded and covered in debris. "Alas!" he said to Pangloss. "Get me some wine and a little oil, I am dying."

"Earthquakes are nothing new," Pangloss replied. "In America the town of Lima experienced the same tremors last year. The same cause, the same effect. There must be an underground vein of sulfur stretching from Lima to Lisbon."

---

a benign deity would have inflicted such suffering. Voltaire wrote an influential poem on the earthquake, "Poème sur la destruction de Lisbonne, ou examen de cet axiome, tout est bien" (Poem on the destruction of Lisbon, or examining the axiom All is for the best).

* In 1629 the custom of *fumi-e,* trampling on the crucifix to prove oneself non-Christian, was introduced in Japan and was used primarily by the Japanese authorities to identify and punish Japanese Christians.

"No doubt," Candide replied. "But for God's sake, a little oil and wine."

"What do you mean, 'no doubt'?" the philosopher asked. "I maintain that it is a proven fact!"

Candide lost consciousness, and Pangloss brought him a little water from a nearby fountain.

The following day, as they made their way through the ruins, they found something to eat and so restored their strength a little. Then they worked alongside the others, tending to the inhabitants who had barely escaped death. Some citizens they helped gave them as good a dinner as they could in such a disaster. It is true that the meal was a somber one. Their dinner companions drenched their bread with tears, but Pangloss consoled them with the assurance that things could not be otherwise. "For things could not be better," he said. "For if there is a volcano in Lisbon, it cannot be someplace else, as it is impossible for things not to be where they are. For all is good."

A small man in black, an agent of the Inquisition who was sitting next to him, said politely, "It seems that the gentleman does not believe in Original Sin. For if all is at its best, there has been neither the Fall of Man nor Eternal Punishment."

"I most humbly beg Your Excellency's pardon," Pangloss replied even more politely. "But the Fall of Man and the ensuing curse necessarily became part of the best of all possible worlds."

"So, sir, you do not believe in liberty?" the agent asked.

"Your Excellency will excuse me," Pangloss replied, "but liberty can survive together with absolute necessity, for it was necessary that we should be free; after all, since will is determined—"

Pangloss was in midsentence when the agent of the Inquisition nodded to his attendant, who was pouring him some port, or rather *oporto.*

Chapter Six

How a fine auto-da-fé was held in order to hinder future earthquakes, and how Candide's buttocks were flogged

After the earthquake that destroyed three quarters of Lisbon, the sages of the land found that the only efficacious way of fending off total ruin was to give the people a fine auto-da-fé. The University of Coimbra concluded that the spectacle of a few people being burned over a slow fire with full ceremony is an infallible formula to prevent the earth from quaking.

They therefore seized a Biscayan convicted of having married his godchild's mother and two Portuguese men who had stripped the bacon off a chicken they were eating.* After the dinner Doctor Pangloss and Candide were put in chains, one for having spoken, the other for having listened with an air of approval. Both were led to separate cells whose air was of an extreme chill, and in which one was never inconvenienced by sunlight. A week later they were clothed in sanbenitos,† their heads adorned with paper miters. On Candide's miter and sanbenito, flames were painted pointing downward, and devils that had neither tails nor talons, but Pangloss's devils sported talons and

* As St. Thomas Aquinas stated in *Summa theologica,* "I may not marry my own child's godmother, nor the mother of my godchild." The implication is that the two Portuguese men are crypto-Jews.

† A garment of sackcloth worn by condemned heretics at an auto-da-fé. The garments with devils were for the impenitent.

tails, and the flames pointed upward. Thus dressed, they marched in a procession and listened to a poignant sermon that was followed by some beautiful *faux-bourdon* chants. During the singing, Candide's bottom was flogged to the beat of the music. The Biscayan and the two men who had refused to eat the bacon off the chicken were burned, and Pangloss was hung, even though this was not customary. The same day the earth quaked once more with a horrifying rumble.

Candide, terrified, dumbfounded, frantic, bleeding all over, and shivering, asked himself, "If this is the best of all possible worlds, what can the others be like? I might accept being flogged—after all I was flogged by the Bulgars too—but O my dear Pangloss, greatest of philosophers! Did I have to see you hung without knowing why? O my dear Anabaptist, best of men! Did you have to be drowned in the port? O Mademoiselle Cunégonde, pearl among women! Did your stomach have to be slashed open?"

As he left, barely able to hold himself upright, having been sermonized, flogged, absolved, and blessed, an old woman accosted him and said, "Take courage, my son. Follow me."

Chapter Seven

How an old woman took care of Candide,
and how he found again what he loved

Candide did not take courage but followed the old woman to a small cottage. She gave him a jar of ointment with which to rub himself and brought him something to eat and drink. She showed him a small bed that was clean enough, next to which lay a full suit of clothes.

"Eat, drink, sleep," the old woman said, "and may Our Lady of Atocha, His Eminence Saint Antonio of Padua, and His Eminence Santiago of Compostela watch over you. I shall return tomorrow."

Candide, still astonished by all he had seen and suffered, and even more astonished by the old woman's charity, tried to kiss her hand.

"It is not my hand you ought to kiss," the old woman said. "I will return tomorrow. Rub yourself with the ointment, eat, and sleep."

Despite all his misfortunes, Candide ate and slept.

The following day the old woman brought him his breakfast, examined his back, and rubbed it herself with another ointment. She then brought him lunch. She returned in the evening with his dinner. The following day she repeated the same ritual.

"Who are you?" Candide kept asking her. "Who has inspired you with so much goodness? How can I show my gratitude?"

The good woman was silent. She returned that evening without bringing any dinner.

"Come with me, and not a word," she said, taking him by the arm and leading him a good quarter of a mile out of the town. They came to a secluded house surrounded by gardens and canals. The old woman knocked on a door. The door was opened. She took Candide up a secret staircase into a gilded chamber, left him sitting on a brocaded sofa, and closed the door behind her as she left. Candide thought he was dreaming. He saw his whole life as a terrible dream but the present moment as a happy one.

The old woman soon reappeared. With some difficulty she was propping up a trembling woman of majestic stature, who was shining with precious stones and covered in a veil.

"Remove the veil," the old woman told Candide. The

young man approached and raised the veil with timid hand. What a moment! What a surprise! He thought he saw Mademoiselle Cunégonde. In fact, he did see her. It was her. His strength failed him. He could not utter a word and fell at her feet. Cunégonde fell onto the sofa. The old woman plied them with fiery spirits. They came to their senses. They spoke to each other: at first with faltering words, disjointed questions and answers, sighs, tears, cries. The old woman suggested they make less noise, then left them alone.

"Is it really you?" Candide asked Cunégonde. "You are alive? I find you again in Portugal! So you were not raped? Your stomach was not ripped open, as the philosopher Pangloss maintained?"

"That did happen," the fair Cunégonde replied. "But one does not always die from two such mishaps."

"But your mother and father, weren't they killed?"

"Only too true," Cunégonde replied, weeping.

"And your brother?"

"My brother was killed, too."

"But why are you in Portugal, and how did you know I was here? By what strange chance did you have me brought to this house?"

"I will tell you everything," Cunégonde replied. "But first you must tell me everything that happened to you since that innocent kiss you gave me, and the kicks you received."

Candide complied with profound respect, and though he was overwhelmed and his buttocks still hurt a little, he told her in the most artless manner and with a trembling and weak voice everything he had endured since the moment of their separation. Cunégonde raised her eyes to Heaven. She shed tears over the deaths of the good Anabaptist and Pangloss, after which she told the following story to Candide, who did not miss a single word and devoured her with his eyes.

Chapter Eight

Cunégonde's story

"I was fast asleep in my bed when it pleased Heaven to send the Bulgars to our fine castle of Thunder-Ten-Tronckh. They butchered my father and brother and hacked my mother to pieces. A big Bulgar, six feet tall, seeing that I had lost consciousness at this spectacle, set about raping me. This brought me around. I came to my senses, I shouted, I struggled, I bit, I scratched. I wanted to rip out that big Bulgar's eyes, unaware that everything taking place at my father's castle was the customary way of doing things. The brute stabbed me in the left side, where I still bear a scar."

"How terrible! I hope to see it," the naïve Candide said.

"You will," Cunégonde replied. "But let me go on."

"Yes, do go on."

She took up the thread of her tale. "A Bulgar captain came in and saw me covered in blood, but the soldier took no notice of him. The captain was furious at the brute's lack of respect toward him and killed him right there on top of me. The captain had me bandaged up and took me to his quarters as a prisoner of war. I laundered the few shirts he had and cooked for him. I must admit that the captain thought me extremely pretty, and I will not deny that he was a most handsome man, with skin that was soft and white. He was, however, somewhat lacking in intellect, and in philosophy too. It was evident he had not been tutored by Doctor Pangloss. At the end of three months, having lost all his money and become sick of me, he sold me to a Jew by the name of Don Issacar, who traded in Holland and Portugal and loved women with a passion. This Jew became quite partial to me but could not triumph over me: I resisted him better than I had the Bulgar soldier. An honorable woman may be raped once, but it only makes her virtue stronger. The Jew brought me to this country house in an attempt to subjugate me. Until then I had thought that there was nothing finer in the world than the castle of Thunder-Ten-Tronckh. My eyes were opened.

"One day, the Grand Inquisitor happened to notice me at mass. He eyed me intently and sent word that he wished to speak to me on a confidential matter. I was led to his palace. I informed him of my birth, and he indicated how beneath my rank it was to belong to an Israelite. An intermediary was sent to Don Issacar, proposing that he cede me to His Eminence the Grand Inquisitor. Don Issacar, a banker to the royal court and a man of influence, would not hear of it. The Inquisitor threatened him with an auto-da-fé. Finally my Jew, intimidated, struck a deal by which the house and I would belong to both of them jointly: The Jew would get Mondays, Wednesdays, and the Sabbath, while the Grand Inquisitor would get the other days of the week. This arrangement has now been in effect for six months. And not without quarrels, for it was often unresolved whether the night of Saturday to Sunday belonged to the old arrangement or the new. As for me, I have so far managed to resist both of them, and I think this is the reason they are still in love with me.

"Finally, to ward off the scourge of the earthquake and to frighten Don Issacar, it pleased His Eminence the Inquisitor to celebrate an auto-da-fé. He did me the honor of inviting me, and I had a very good seat indeed. The ladies were served refreshments between mass and the execution. To tell you the truth, I was horrified to see the burning of the two Jews and the good Biscayan who had married the mother of his godchild. But imagine my surprise, my fright, my grief, when I saw a figure in a sanbenito and miter that resembled Pangloss! I rubbed my eyes in disbelief, watched carefully, and saw him hanged. I swooned. Scarcely had I regained consciousness when I saw you stripped quite naked. It was the peak of horror, consternation, grief, and despair! I tell you, quite in truth, that your skin is of an even more exquisite white and rosiness than that of my Bulgar captain. This sight redoubled all the feelings that were overcoming me, that were consuming me. I cried out. I wanted to shout, 'Stop, you barbarians!' But my voice failed me, and my shouts would have been pointless. When your buttocks had been well flogged, I exclaimed, 'How is it possible that sweet Candide and wise Pangloss are here in Lisbon, one to receive a hundred lashes of the whip, and the other to be hanged by order of His Eminence the Grand Inquisitor, whose beloved I am? Pangloss deceived me most cruelly when he told me that everything is for the best in this world!'

"I was frantic, distraught, quite beside myself, and ready to collapse and die of weakness, my mind filled with the slaughter of my father, mother, and brother, the insolence of my foul Bulgar soldier and how he stabbed me, my servitude, my work as a cook, my Bulgar captain, my foul Don Issacar, my abominable inquisitor, the hanging of Doctor Pangloss, the great *faux-bourdon* Miserere during which your buttocks were flogged, and most of all I called to mind the kiss you gave me behind the screen the day I saw you for the last time. I praised God for having brought you back to me through so many ordeals. I told my old servant to take care of you and bring you here as soon as possible. I am very pleased with how she carried out my commission. I have enjoyed the inexpressible pleasure of once again seeing you, hearing you, and speaking to you. Your hunger must be rapacious indeed. I have quite an appetite. Let's have some supper."

So the two of them sat down at table, and after dinner they returned to the fine aforementioned sofa. And that is where they were when Signor Don Issacar, one of the masters of the house, walked in. It was the Sabbath. He had come to enjoy his rights and to articulate his tender love.

Chapter Nine

What became of Cunégonde, Candide, the Grand Inquisitor, and a Jew

This Issacar was the most choleric Hebrew that Israel had seen since the Babylonian Captivity.*

"What!" he shouted. "You Galilean harlot! To share you with His Eminence the Inquisitor is not enough, now I must also share you with this rogue?" While saying this he drew a long dagger he always carried and, believing Candide unarmed, threw himself upon him. But the old woman had given our good Westphalian a fine sword along with the suit of clothes. Notwithstanding the sweetness of his disposition, he now drew the sword, and the Israelite was stretched out dead on the tiles at the fair Cunégonde's feet.

* The Babylonian Captivity was the deportation of the Jews to Babylon by the Babylonian king Nebuchadrezzar, c. 630–561 B.C.E.

"Holy Virgin!" she exclaimed. "What will become of us? A man killed in my house! If the law comes, we'll be finished!"

"Had Pangloss not been hanged," Candide said, "he would have given us good advice in these extreme circumstances, for he was a great philosopher. As he is not at hand, we will have to consult the old woman."

The old woman was very wise and had just begun giving her opinion when another little door opened. It was an hour past midnight, the beginning of Sunday, a day that belonged to the Grand Inquisitor. He entered and saw the flogged Candide with sword in hand, a dead man lying stretched out on the floor, a frightened Cunégonde, and the old woman doling out advice.

This is what passed through Candide's mind and how he reasoned: "If this saintly man calls for help, he will certainly have me burned. He might well do the same to Cunégonde. He did have me pitilessly flogged. He is my rival. I have just killed one man. This is no time to hesitate." This reasoning was clear and rapid. Without giving the inquisitor time to recover from his surprise, Candide drove his sword through him and threw him on the floor next to the Jew. "Oh, God, another one!" Cunégonde exclaimed. "This will not be forgiven. We will be excommunicated! Our final hour has struck! How could you, who were born with such a gentle disposition, kill within two minutes a Jew and a prelate?"

"Fair Cunégonde," Candide replied, "when a man is in love, is jealous, and has been flogged by the Inquisition, he is no longer himself."

The old woman spoke up again. "There are three Andalusian horses in the stable, with their saddles and bridles. Let the valiant Candide prepare them. Madame has the gold coins and the diamonds. Let us quickly jump on our saddles, though I can only sit on one buttock, and flee to Cádiz. The weather is the most agreeable in the world, and it is such a pleasure to travel in the coolness of the night."

Candide immediately saddled the three horses. Cunégonde, the old woman, and he covered thirty miles in a stretch. As they rode away, the Santa Hermandad arrived at the house.* They buried His Eminence in a fine church and threw Issacar onto a garbage dump.

Candide, Cunégonde, and the old woman had already reached the small town of Avacena in the middle of the Sierra Morena. They were at an inn, deep in conversation.

Chapter Ten

The distress in which Candide, Cunégonde, and the old woman arrive at Cádiz, and their embarkation

"But who could have stolen my diamonds and money?" Cunégonde said, weeping. "What will we live on? What will we do? Where can we find inquisitors or Jews who will give me more?"

"Alas," the old woman said. "I strongly suspect the reverend Franciscan Father who was staying yesterday at our inn in Badajoz. God keep me from making a rash judgment, but he came into our room twice and left the inn long before we did."

"Alas," said Candide. "Good Pangloss often proved that the things of this world belong to all men in common, and that every man has the same right to them. But according

* The Santa Hermandad (Holy Brotherhood) was a Catholic military constabulary set up in the fifteenth century.

to these principles, the Franciscan ought to have left us enough to complete our journey. So you have nothing left at all, dear Cunégonde?"

"Not a copper *maravedi,*" she replied.

"What should we do?" Candide exclaimed.

"Why not sell one of the horses?" the old woman said. "I can ride sidesaddle behind Mademoiselle—as I can only sit on one buttock—and that way we can reach Cádiz."

There was a Benedictine prior at the inn where they were staying, and he bought the horse cheaply. Candide, Cunégonde, and the old woman rode through Lucena, Chillas, and Lebrija, and finally arrived in Cádiz. Troops were being assembled and a fleet equipped with the aim of bringing reason to a reverend who had been accused of inciting one of the tribes of Indians near the town of San Sacramento to revolt against the Kings of Spain and Portugal.* Candide, having served in the Bulgar ranks, executed Bulgar drills before the general of the small army with such grace, speed, dexterity, pride, and agility that he was given an infantry company to command. So there he was, a captain. He embarked with Mademoiselle Cunégonde, the old woman, two valets, and the two Andalusian horses that had belonged to His Eminence the Grand Inquisitor of Portugal.

Throughout the voyage they reasoned about the philosophy of poor Pangloss. "We are traveling to another world," Candide said, "and it is there, without a doubt, that all is well. For it must be admitted that one has cause to grumble about what goes on physically and morally in ours."

* The Jesuits had organized Guarani villages in Paraguay into autonomous communities to resist destructive Spanish colonization and exploitation. In 1750 Spain ceded San Sacramento to Portugal, triggering uprisings by the Guarani communities that were to be evicted from their land.

"I love you with all my heart," Cunégonde said, "but my spirit is still completely shaken by everything I have seen and endured."

"It will all be fine," Candide replied. "The sea of this new world is already better than any of the seas of Europe. This sea is calmer, and the winds more constant. It is certainly this new world that is the best of all possible worlds."

"God grant that it be so!" Cunégonde replied. "But I was so terribly unhappy in my world that my heart is almost despairing of hope."

"You complain," the old woman said to them. "But alas! You have not suffered misfortunes to compare with mine."

Cunégonde could barely keep herself from laughing. She found it quite amusing that the old woman would claim to be more unhappy than she. "Alas, my dear woman," Cunégonde said, "unless you have been raped by two Bulgars, stabbed two times in the stomach, had two of your castles demolished, and unless you had two fathers and two mothers butchered before your very eyes and saw two lovers whipped at an auto-da-fé, I cannot see how you can possibly claim to have outdone me. Especially if you add to this that I was born a baroness with seventy-two heraldic quarterings of noble lineage, and was subsequently reduced to being a cook."

"Mademoiselle," the old woman replied, "you are not aware of my pedigree. And were I to show you my bottom, you would not speak as you do but would immediately abandon your claim."

This statement aroused much curiosity in Cunégonde and Candide. This is what the old woman told them:

Chapter Eleven

The old woman's story

"I did not always have blurry, red-rimmed eyes. My nose did not always touch my chin, nor was I always a servant. I am the daughter of Pope Urban X and the Princess of Palestrina.* I was raised up to the age of fourteen in a palace for which your German barons' castles could not have served as stables. A single one of my dresses was worth more than all the splendors of Westphalia. I grew in beauty, graces, and talents, surrounded by pleasures, deference, and expectations. I was already inspiring love. My breasts were forming, and what breasts! White, firm, and chiseled like those of the Venus de Medici. And what eyes! What eyelids! What black eyebrows! The flames that burned in both my pupils eclipsed the brightness of the stars, as our local poets used to tell me. The women who dressed and undressed me were overcome with ecstasy when they chanced to view me from the front and from behind, and there was not a man who would not have wanted to be in their place.

"I was betrothed to a sovereign prince of Massa-Carrara. And what a prince! As handsome as I was beautiful, filled with sweetness and charm, sparkling with wit, and burning with love. And I loved him as one loves for the first time: with idolatry, with infatuation. The wedding preparations began. What unparalleled pomp and splendor! There were endless feasts, tournaments, and opera buffas, and all

* [Voltaire's footnote] Observe the extreme discretion of the author: There never was a Pope Urban X, the author having qualms about conferring a bastard on an actual pope. What circumspection, what delicacy of conscience!

of Italy wrote sonnets to me, not one of which, however, was of any note. My moment of happiness was already within reach when an old marquise who had been my prince's lover invited him to partake of some chocolate with her. He died in less than two hours, in terrible convulsions. But that was a mere trifle. My mother—in despair, though less afflicted than I—wanted to flee from this place of misery for a while. She had a very fine estate near Gaeta. We set out in one of the principality's galleys that was gilded like the altar of St. Peter's in Rome, when suddenly a corsair from Salé converged on us and boarded our vessel. Our soldiers defended themselves like soldiers of the Pope: they fell to their knees, threw down their weapons, and begged the corsair for absolution *in articulo mortis*.*

"They were immediately stripped naked as apes, as was my mother, her maids of honor, and I. The diligence with which those gentlemen undress people is quite remarkable. But what surprised me most was that they all poked their fingers in a certain place where we women will usually allow only cannulas to be inserted.† I thought this ceremony quite strange (one hardly knows what to make of things when one has never been out of one's country before). I soon learned that they did this to see if we had any diamonds hidden there. It is a custom established from time immemorial among civilized nations pirating on the high seas. I heard that the Knights of Malta never fail in this practice when they capture a Turkish man or woman. It is one of the laws of the rights of man that has always been adhered to.

* *In articulo mortis* is liturgical Latin meaning "in the article of death"—at the moment of death.

† A cannula is an enema tube.

"I cannot begin to tell you how hard it is for a young princess to be sent as a slave to Morocco with her mother. I am sure you can imagine what we had to endure on that corsair vessel. My mother was still very beautiful, while our maids of honor and even our simplest chambermaids had more charms than could be found in all of Africa. As for myself, I was ravishing. I was a beauty, I was grace itself, and I was a virgin. I didn't remain one for long. The flower reserved for the handsome Prince of Massa-Carrara was ravished by the corsair captain. He was a repulsive Negro, who was actually under the impression that he was doing me a great honor. To be sure, the Princess of Palestrina and I had to be very strong to bear all our sufferings until we arrived in Morocco. But let us pass over that. These are things so commonplace that they are not worth mentioning.

"Morocco was bathed in blood when we arrived. All fifty of Emperor Moulay-Ismail's sons had their own factions, which in effect resulted in fifty civil wars: blacks against blacks, blacks against browns, browns against browns, mulattoes against mulattoes.* There was never-ending carnage throughout the empire.

"No sooner had we disembarked than some blacks from a rival faction to that of our corsair arrived, intent on making off with his spoils. After his diamonds and gold, we were his most precious possessions. I witnessed a fight the likes of which would never be seen in your European climes. The blood of northern people is not fiery enough. They do not have the kind of hunger for women common in Africa. It seems that you Europeans have milk in your veins. Vitriol and fire flows through the veins of the inhabi-

* Moulay-Ismail, 1645–1727, ruled Morocco for fifty years. After his death, a power struggle among his sons (he was reputed to have had 700) led to civil war.

tants of the Atlas Mountains and the neighboring countries. They fought with the rage of the lions, tigers, and serpents of those places, to determine to whom we would belong. A Moor seized my mother by her right hand, my captain's lieutenant seized her by the left; a Moorish soldier grabbed hold of one of her legs, and a pirate grabbed hold of the other. Almost all our girls were being pulled this way by four soldiers. My captain kept me hidden behind him. He was wielding his scimitar, killing all in the path of his rage. In the end, I saw all our Italians and my mother ripped to pieces, slashed, and massacred by the monsters who were wrangling over us. My fellow captives and our captors, the soldiers, sailors, blacks, browns, whites, mulattoes, and finally my captain, were all killed, while I was left dying on a heap of corpses. It is common knowledge that such scenes were taking place over an area of more than three hundred leagues all around, without anyone neglecting the five prayers a day prescribed by Mohammed.

"With great effort, I disentangled myself from the mound of bleeding corpses and dragged myself beneath a big orange tree that stood on the bank of a nearby stream. There I collapsed from fear, exhaustion, horror, despair, and hunger. Soon after, my overwhelmed senses fell into a deep sleep that was more unconsciousness than rest. I was in this state of weakness and insensibility, between life and death, when I felt something pressing and wriggling against my body. I opened my eyes and saw a handsome white man, sighing and muttering between his teeth, '*O che sciagura d'essere senza coglioni!*' "*

* "Oh, what a calamity to be without testicles!" (Italian).

Chapter Twelve

The continuation of the old woman's misfortunes

"Astonished and delighted at hearing the language of my native land, and no less surprised at the words this man had uttered, I replied that there were greater misfortunes than the one of which he was complaining. I informed him in a few words of the horrors I had suffered and then fell back into a faint. He carried me to a nearby house, had me fed and put to bed, cared for me, consoled me, said many flattering things, told me that he had never seen anything as beautiful as I, and that never before had he so regretted losing that which no one could restore to him.

" 'I was born in Naples,' he told me. 'Two or three thousand boys are caponized there every year. Some die, others acquire a voice more beautiful than that of any woman, others go on to govern nations.* I was operated on with great success and became a singer in the chapel of Her Highness the Princess of Palestrina.'

" 'My mother's chapel?' I exclaimed.

" 'Your mother's chapel?' he replied, weeping. 'Then you must be the young princess I tutored to the age of six, who even then was promising to become as beautiful as you!'

" 'I am she! My mother is lying some four hundred paces away, torn into four pieces beneath a heap of corpses!'

"I told him everything that had happened to me, and he told me his adventures. He told me how he had been sent to the Sultan of Morocco by a Christian nation in order to

* A reference to the famous castrato singer Farinelli, 1705–1782, who had become one of the most powerful men in Spanish politics.

sign a treaty, under which the king would be supplied with gunpowder, cannons, and ships to help destroy the commerce of other Christian nations.*

" 'As my mission has been accomplished,' the honest eunuch said, 'I am embarking for Ceuta and will take you back to Italy. *Ma che sciagura d'essere senza coglioni!*'

"I thanked him with tears of tenderness—but instead of taking me to Italy he took me to Algiers, where he sold me to the dey of the province. No sooner was I sold than the plague that had swept through Africa, Asia, and Europe arrived with a vengeance in Algiers. You have seen earthquakes, Mademoiselle, but have you ever had the plague?"

"Never," the young baroness replied.

"If you had," the old woman continued, "you would have to admit that it ranks well above an earthquake. The plague is extremely common in Africa. It struck me. Imagine the predicament for a daughter of a pope, just fifteen years old, who within a period of three months had endured poverty and slavery, had been raped practically every day, seen her mother quartered, and endured hunger and war, only to die plague-ridden in Algiers. And yet I did not die. But my eunuch and the dey and almost all the harem of Algiers did perish.

"After the first ravages of this terrible plague had passed, the slaves of the dey were sold. A trader bought me and took me to Tunis, where he sold me to another trader, who resold me in Tripoli. From Tripoli I was resold to Alexandria, from Alexandria I was resold to Smyrna, and from Smyrna to Constantinople. I finally became the property of an aga of the janissaries, who was soon ordered to

* In his historical work *Le siècle de Louis XIV* (*The Age of Louis XIV*), Chapter 13, Voltaire describes Portugal's attempts to ally itself with Sultan Moulay-Ismail of Morocco at the start of the War of the Spanish Succession, 1701–1713.

go defend Azov against the Russians, who had laid siege to it.*

"The aga, a very gallant man, took his whole harem with him, putting us up in a small fort on the Maeotian Marshes under the guard of two black eunuchs and twenty soldiers. The Russians were being killed most prodigiously, but they were paying us back in kind. Azov was put to fire and sword, and neither the women nor the old were spared. Only our little fort was still holding out. The enemy wanted to starve us into surrendering, but the twenty janissaries had sworn an oath that they would never surrender. The extremity of hunger to which they were reduced compelled them, for fear of breaking their oath, to eat our two eunuchs. Within a few days, they determined to eat the women.

"We had an imam, a very pious and compassionate man, who preached a fine sermon in which he persuaded them not to kill us outright. 'Chop off one buttock from each of these ladies, and you can make a fine feast of it. And if in a few days you need more, you can be sure of the same portion again. Heaven will thank you for showing such charity, and you will be saved.'

"He was very eloquent, and they were persuaded. We underwent this terrible operation. The imam smeared us with the same balm that is applied to children who have just been circumcised. All of us were on the point of death.

"No sooner had the janissaries finished the meal we had furnished them than the Russians arrived in flat boats. Not a single janissary escaped. The Russians did not pay the least attention to the state we were in. There are French

* Czar Peter the Great besieged the Turkish fortress of Azov from 1695 to 1697. While writing *Candide*, Voltaire was working on his book *Histoire de l'empire de Russie sous Pierre le Grand* (*The History of the Russian Empire under Peter the Great*). The siege is described in chapter 8.

surgeons everywhere, and one of them, a very skillful man, took care of us. He cured us, and—I will remember this till the day I die—when my wounds had healed he made certain suggestions to me. Furthermore, he told us all to take heart, assuring us that the like happened in many sieges, and that it was the law of war.

"As soon as my companions were able to walk, they were sent to Moscow. As for me, I ended up as part of the spoils of a boyar who made me his gardener and gave me twenty lashes a day. But two years later this gentleman was racked on a wheel with some thirty other boyars on account of some court intrigue, and I turned this stroke of fortune to my advantage and fled.* I crossed the whole of Russia. I worked for a long time as a maid at an inn in Riga, then in Rostock, Wismar, Leipzig, Kassel, Utrecht, Leiden, the Hague, and Rotterdam. I grew old in misery and disgrace, with but half a bottom, never forgetting that I was the daughter of a pope. A hundred times I wanted to kill myself, but I was still in love with life. This ridiculous weakness is perhaps one of our most sinister tendencies. For is there anything more foolish than to insist on carrying a burden that one can drop at any moment? To live in constant fear, and yet still hold on to life? To caress the serpent that is devouring you until it has eaten your heart?

"In the countries through which fate made me wander, and in the inns where I worked, I have seen an inordinate number of people who detested their existence. And yet I saw only twelve who voluntarily put an end to their misery: three Negroes, four Englishmen, four Genevans, and a German professor by the name of Robeck.† I ended up as

* A reference to the Revolt of the Streltsy (Russian guardsmen) in June 1698.

† Johann Robeck, 1672–1739, was a German philosopher who wrote an influential philosophical defense of suicide.

maid to the Jew Don Issacar. He appointed me your servant, dear lady. I attached myself to your destiny and became more concerned with your lot than with mine. I would not even have spoken to you of my misfortunes had you not vexed me a little and if it were not customary on a ship to tell stories to relieve the boredom. You see, Mademoiselle, I have experience, I know the world. To pass the time, why don't you ask every passenger to tell you his life's story? And if there is a single one among them who has never cursed his life, who has not often told himself that he was the unhappiest of men, then you may throw me overboard, headfirst!"

Chapter Thirteen

How Candide was forced to part with the fair Cunégonde and the old woman

Having heard the old woman's tale, the fair Cunégonde paid her all the reverence due a person of her rank and merit. She followed the old woman's advice and asked the passengers, one by one, to tell her their adventures. Cunégonde and Candide had to admit that the old woman was right. "It is such a pity," Candide said, "that wise Pangloss was hanged contrary to the custom of an auto-da-fé. He would have told us wonderful things about the physical evil and the moral evil that cover land and sea, and I feel I would have mettle enough to raise a few respectful objections."

The ship sailed on, each passenger telling his tale. They landed in Buenos Aires. Cunégonde, Captain Candide, and the old woman went to see the governor, Don Fernando d'Ibarra y Figueroa y Mascarenes y Lampourdos y Souza.

This gentleman had all the pride befitting a man bearing so many names. He spoke with such noble derision, carried his nose so high, raised his voice so mercilessly, affected such an imposing tone, and adopted such a haughty gait that all who greeted him had to suppress the urge to strike him. He loved women with a passion. Cunégonde seemed to him the most beautiful woman he had ever seen. The first thing he did was to ask whether she might be the captain's wife. The manner in which he posed this question alarmed Candide. He did not dare say that she was his wife because, in fact, she was not. He did not dare maintain that she was his sister, because she wasn't his sister either. Though this diplomatic lie had been quite the fashion among the ancients and could prove useful among the moderns too, Candide's soul was too pure to misrepresent the truth.*

"Mademoiselle Cunégonde has done me the great honor of accepting my hand in marriage," Candide said, "and we beg Your Excellency to favor us with condescending to preside over the ceremony."

Don Fernando d'Ibarra y Figueroa y Mascarenes y Lampourdos y Souza twirled his mustaches haughtily and with a mordant smile ordered Captain Candide to go inspect his company. Candide obeyed. The governor remained alone with Mademoiselle Cunégonde. He declared his passion for her and announced that he would marry her the following day in the rites of the church, or in any other way that her charming self might please. Cunégonde asked him for a quarter of an hour to gather her thoughts, to dis-

* In the Bible, both Abraham and his son Isaac presented their wives as their sisters. In Genesis 12, Abraham's wife Sarah became the pharaoh's concubine, and in Genesis 20 she became the concubine of King Abimelech of Gerar. In Genesis 26, Isaac presents his wife Rebecca as his sister.

cuss the matter with the old woman and come to a decision.

The old woman said to Cunégonde, "Mademoiselle, you have seventy-two heraldic quarterings of noble lineage but are without a brass coin to your name. You have it in your power to be the wife of the greatest nobleman in South America, who has a splendid mustache. Are you in a position in which you can flaunt the luxury of unflinching fidelity? You were raped by the Bulgars; a Jew and an inquisitor have enjoyed your favors. Misfortunes bestow certain rights. I confess that were I in your position, I would not harbor the least scruple at marrying the governor, and thereby securing Captain Candide's fortune."

As the old woman spoke with all the prudence that age and experience bring with them, a small ship was seen pulling into the harbor. It brought a Spanish magistrate and some of his officers, for this is what had happened: The old woman had guessed correctly that a long-sleeved Franciscan had stolen Cunégonde's gold and jewels in the town of Badajoz during her flight with Candide. This monk had tried to sell a few of the stones to a jeweler, who had recognized them as belonging to the Grand Inquisitor. Before he was hanged, the Franciscan confessed that he had stolen them, stating who he had stolen them from and where these people were heading. The authorities already knew of Cunégonde's and Candide's escape. They were followed to Cádiz, and a ship was promptly dispatched in pursuit. The ship had now arrived in the port of Buenos Aires. Word had spread that a magistrate was about to disembark and that the murderers of His Eminence the Grand Inquisitor were being pursued. The shrewd old woman saw in an instant what had to be done. "You cannot flee," she told Cunégonde, "but you have nothing to fear. You were not the one who killed His Eminence. And moreover, the governor loves you and would not permit them to mistreat you. You must stay."

The old woman then hurried off to find Candide. "Flee!" she told him. "Or you will be burned within the hour."

There wasn't a moment to lose. But how could he part from Cunégonde, and where should he flee to?

Chapter Fourteen

How Candide and Cacambo were received by the Jesuits of Paraguay

Candide had brought with him a valet from Cádiz of a kind quite common on the coasts of Spain and its colonies. This valet was a quarter Spanish, born of a half-breed in Tucumán. He had been a choirboy, a sacristan, a sailor, a monk, a middleman, a soldier, and a lackey. His name was Cacambo, and he truly loved his master, for his master truly was a good man. He saddled the two Andalusian horses as fast as he could.

"Hurry, Master! We must follow the old woman's advice. Let us flee without looking back!"

Candide wept bitterly. "O my beloved Cunégonde! Must I abandon you just as the governor is about to preside over our wedding? O Cunégonde, brought here from afar, what will become of you?"

"She will become whatever she can," Cacambo replied. "Women always find a way. God sees to that. Let us flee!"

"Where are you taking me? Where are we going? What are we to do without Cunégonde?" Candide asked.

"By Santiago de Compostela!" Cacambo replied. "We were going to war against the Jesuits. Let us go to war alongside them. I know the roads here well enough, and I will take you to their kingdom. They will be delighted to welcome a captain who drills troops in the Bulgar fashion. You will make a prodigious fortune. If you cannot get what you desire in one world, you must get it in another. It is always a great pleasure to see and do new things."

"So you have been to Paraguay before?" Candide asked.

"Indeed I have," Cacambo replied. "I was a lackey at the Collegium of the Assumption, and I know the government of Los Padres as well as I know the streets of Cádiz.* A most remarkable government! Their kingdom is already more than three hundred leagues in diameter and is divided into thirty provinces. Los Padres own everything, while the people own nothing. It is a masterpiece of reason and justice. If you ask me, there is nothing as divine as Los Padres, who are waging war on the Kings of Spain and Portugal here in the Americas, while in Europe they are these kings' confessors. And they kill the Spaniards here, while in Madrid they send them to Heaven. It's enchanting! Let's hurry. You will be the happiest of men. How pleased Los Padres will be when they find that they are getting a captain who knows the Bulgar drills!"

As soon as they reached the first outpost, Cacambo informed the guard that a captain wished to speak to His Grace the Commandant. Word was sent to headquarters. A Paraguayan officer ran and knelt at the feet of the commandant to inform him of the news. Candide and Cacambo were disarmed and their two Andalusian horses taken away. The two strangers walked between two rows of soldiers, at the head of which stood the commandant, a Jesuit's three-

* Los Padres refers to the Jesuits who ruled parts of Paraguay from 1607 to 1767. In the 1750s it was rumored that a Jesuit had been crowned king of Paraguay.

cornered hat on his head, his cassock drawn up, a sword at his side, and a halberd in his hand. He made a sign, and twenty-four soldiers immediately encircled the newcomers. A sergeant informed them that they had to wait. The commandant was not permitted to speak to them, as the Reverend Father Provincial did not allow Spaniards to speak to anyone unless he himself was present, nor did he allow foreigners to stay in the country for longer than three hours.

"And where is the Reverend Father Provincial?" Cacambo asked.

"He has finished mass and is now reviewing the troops," the sergeant replied. "You will not be able to kiss his spurs before three hours from now."

"But the captain, who like me is dying of hunger, is not a Spaniard. He is a German. Could we not have lunch while we are waiting for His Reverence?"

The sergeant immediately went to report this conversation to the commandant.

"God be praised!" His Grace the Commandant said. "As he is a German, I can speak to him. Have him brought to my arbor."

Candide was immediately taken to a leafy bower adorned with an exquisite colonnade of green and gilded marble, and trellises that sheltered parrots, colibris, hummingbirds, guinea fowl, and the rarest species of birds. An excellent meal was laid out on golden dishes. While in the fields the Paraguayans were eating maize from wooden bowls in the blazing sun, the Reverend Father Commandant rested in his arbor.

He was an extremely handsome young man, with a full face, a fair complexion, flushed cheeks, pleasantly arched eyebrows, bright eyes, pink ears, vermilion lips, and a proud bearing that was neither that of a Spaniard nor of a Jesuit.

Candide and Cacambo were given back their weapons and their two Andalusian horses. Cacambo fed them oats near the arbor, as he wanted to be near in case of a surprise attack.

Candide kissed the hem of the commandant's cassock, after which they sat down to table.

"So, you are a German?" the Jesuit asked him in that tongue.

"Yes, Reverend Father," Candide replied.

At these words, the two men looked at each other with extreme surprise and an emotion they were unable to master.

"And from which German province might you be?" the Jesuit asked.

"From the foul province of Westphalia," Candide replied. "I was born at the castle of Thunder-Ten-Tronckh."

"God in Heaven! Is it possible?" the commandant cried out.

"What a miracle!" Candide exclaimed.

"Can it be you?" the commandant said.

"This cannot be!" Candide said.

They both fell back in their chairs in amazement, embraced, and wept streams of tears.

"Can it be you, Reverend Father? You, the brother of the fair Cunégonde? You, who were killed by the Bulgars? You, the son of the baron? You, a Jesuit in Paraguay? I must confess, this world is a strange place! O Pangloss! Pangloss! Had you not been hanged, how happy you would be!"

The commandant dismissed the black slaves and the Paraguayans who were serving drinks in goblets of rock crystal. He thanked God and Saint Ignatius a thousand times. He clasped Candide in his arms. Their faces were drenched with tears.

"You will be even more astonished, moved, and beside

yourself," Candide said, "when I tell you that Mademoiselle Cunégonde, your sister who you thought was disemboweled, is in the best of health."

"Where?"

"Nearby, with the Governor of Buenos Aires. And to think I came from Cádiz to wage war on you."

Every word they spoke in this long conversation piled wonder upon wonder. Their souls danced upon their tongues, listened in their ears, and sparkled in their eyes. As they were Germans, they sat at table for a long time. While they waited for the Reverend Father Provincial, this is what the commandant said to his dear Candide:

Chapter Fifteen

How Candide killed the brother of his beloved Cunégonde

"To my dying hour I shall always have before me that terrible day on which I saw my father and mother killed and my sister raped. When the Bulgars withdrew, my adored sister Cunégonde was nowhere to be found. I was put in a cart along with my mother and father, two servants, and three little boys who had also been butchered, and we were taken away to be buried in a Jesuit chapel, two leagues from the castle of my forefathers. A Jesuit threw some holy water on us. It was horribly salty. A few drops got into my eyes, and the Jesuit noticed that my eyelids were twitching. He put his hand on my heart and felt it beating. I was rescued, and within three weeks my injuries had healed without a trace. As you know, my dear Candide, I was very handsome, and I grew even handsomer. Reverend Father Croust, the rector of the house, also began to feel a most tender friendship for me.* He gave me a novice's habit.

A short time later I was sent to Rome. The Father General happened to be looking for young German Jesuit recruits. The Jesuit monarchs of Paraguay engage as few Spanish Jesuits as possible. They prefer foreigners, whom they believe they can lord over more easily. The Reverend Father General considered me suitable to labor in that vineyard. We set out: a Pole, a Tyrolian, and I. On my arrival in Paraguay I was honored with a subdeaconship and a lieutenancy. Today I am a colonel and a priest. We are preparing a most hearty reception for the troops of the King of Spain. I assure you that they will be both excommunicated and defeated! Providence has sent you here to assist us. But is it true that my beloved sister, Cunégonde, is with the Governor of Buenos Aires nearby?"

Candide assured him with a solemn oath that nothing could be more true. Their tears began to flow once more.

The baron could not desist from embracing Candide. He called him his brother, his savior. "Ah, my dear Candide," he said, "perhaps you and I can enter the city together as victors and reclaim my sister."

"That is my desire," said Candide. "For I was intent on marrying her, and I still am."

"You insolent rascal!" the baron replied. "You have the temerity to think of marrying my sister with her seventy-two heraldic quarterings of noble lineage? What insolence to dare speak to me of such a rash scheme!"

Candide, petrified at these words, said, "My Reverend Father, all the heraldic quarters of the world have nothing to do with this. I have dragged your sister from the clutches

* François-Antoine Croust, an opponent of Voltaire, was an influential Jesuit whose brother was the confessor of Louis XVI's mother.

of a Jew and an inquisitor. She is quite indebted to me, and wishes to marry me. Doctor Pangloss always told me that men are equal, and I am intent on marrying her."

"We shall see about that, you rascal!" the Jesuit Baron of Thunder-Ten-Tronckh said, hitting Candide across the face with the flat of his blade. Candide immediately drew his sword and plunged it to the hilt into the Jesuit baron's stomach. But as he pulled out his smoking blade, he began to weep. "Alas! My God!" he said. "I have killed my former master, friend, and brother-in-law! I am the best man in the world, but I have already killed three men, and two of them were priests."

Cacambo, who had been standing watch at the door of the arbor, came running in.

"There is nothing we can do but sell our lives dearly," Candide said. "They will doubtless enter the arbor. We must die with our weapons drawn."

Cacambo, who had been in a few scrapes in his time, kept a cool head. He removed the Jesuit cassock from the baron, had Candide wear it along with the dead man's three-cornered hat, and bade him mount his horse. All this happened in the blink of an eye.

"Let us gallop away, Master. Everyone will take you for a Jesuit carrying military orders. We will cross the border before they can chase us down." He was already riding off as he spoke these words and shouted in Spanish, "Make way! Make way for the Colonel Reverend Father!"

Chapter Sixteen

*What happened to the two travelers with two girls, two monkeys, and the savages called the Orejones**

Candide and his valet had crossed the border, but still nobody in the camp had discovered the death of the German Jesuit. Clever Cacambo had taken care to fill his saddlebags with bread, chocolate, ham, fruit, and a few pints of wine. With their Andalusian horses, they penetrated deep into an unknown country, where they could not discover a single path. At last a fine stretch of grassland crisscrossed by streams opened out before them. The two travelers stopped to let their horses graze. Cacambo urged his master to eat and set him an example.

"How can you expect me to eat ham," Candide said, "when I have killed His Lordship's son and am thus condemned never again to see the fair Cunégonde? What is the point of prolonging my miserable days, when I must drag them out far away from her in remorse and despair? And what will the *Journal de Trévoux* say?"† Though he spoke these words, he did not shun his food. The sun was setting. The two lost travelers heard a few faint cries that they assumed were made by women. They could not tell if they were cries of pain or joy, but they jumped to their feet with the distress and fright everything in an unknown country inspires. The cries came from two utterly unclothed maidens, who were running nimbly along the edge

* The Orejones were a Peruvian tribe described by Garcilaso de la Vega, 1539–1616, in his influential work *Royal Commentaries of the Incas.*

† The *Journal de Trévoux* was a Jesuit journal founded in 1701.

of the grassland, followed by two monkeys who were biting them in the buttocks. Candide was moved to pity. He had learned to shoot in the Bulgar ranks and could have hit a hazelnut in a bush without disturbing a leaf. He took his double-barreled Spanish rifle, fired, and killed the two monkeys.

"God be praised, my dear Cacambo! I have delivered the two poor maidens from a great peril. If I have committed a sin by killing an inquisitor and a Jesuit, then I have redeemed myself by saving the lives of these two creatures. They might well be young ladies of breeding, and this escapade might secure us great advantages in this country." He was going to continue, but his tongue was paralyzed when he saw the girls embrace the monkeys tenderly, cry bitter tears over their bodies, and fill the air with the most sorrowful lamentations.

"I never expected to witness such goodness of soul," Candide said to Cacambo.

"A fine piece of work, Master! You have just killed these young maidens' lovers."

"Their lovers! Can it be? You are making fun of me, Cacambo! How can I believe you?"

"My dear master," Cacambo replied. "Everything always surprises you. Why do you find it so strange that in some countries there might be monkeys who can attain the good favors of a lady? They are a quarter human, as I am a quarter Spanish."

"Alas!" Candide said. "I remember Doctor Pangloss saying that similar mishaps have occurred in the past, and that such interbreedings have brought about Aegipans,* fauns, and satyrs, and that many great figures of antiquity had seen them. But I always took them for fables."

* In Greek mythology, the Aegipan was half goat, half man.

"This must surely convince you that it's all true," Cacambo said. "And you can see how people act who have not enjoyed a certain upbringing. The only thing that worries me is that these ladies might cause us trouble."

These sound deliberations swayed Candide to leave the grassland and enter deep into a forest. There he dined with Cacambo, and after they had cursed the Inquisitor of Portugal, the Governor of Buenos Aires, and the baron, they both fell asleep on a patch of moss. When they woke up, they could not move. The reason for this was that during the night the Orejones, the inhabitants of these parts, to whom the two ladies had denounced them, had tied them up with ropes made of bark. They were surrounded by some fifty Orejones, who were completely naked and armed with arrows, clubs, and stone axes. Some were heating a large cauldron, others were preparing spits, and all were shouting, "He's a Jesuit, he's a Jesuit! We will be avenged and have a feast! Let's eat some Jesuit, let's eat some Jesuit!"

"I told you, dear Master, that these two maidens would play a foul trick on us," Cacambo said sadly.

Candide, seeing the cauldron and the spits, exclaimed, "We will certainly be roasted or boiled! Oh, what would Doctor Pangloss say were he to see what a state of nature is about? Granted all is for the best, but I admit that it is quite cruel to have lost Mademoiselle Cunégonde and to be roasted on a spit by Orejones."

Cacambo was not a man to lose his head. "Do not despair," he said to the despondent Candide. "I understand a little of this people's gibberish. I will talk to them."

"Do not forget to point out how frightfully inhuman it is to cook people, and how unchristian."

"Gentlemen," Cacambo said. "I see you are intent on eating a Jesuit today. That is good. Nothing is more just than to treat one's enemy like that. The law of nature teaches us to kill our neighbor, and that is what is done all over the world. If my people do not exercise the right to eat our neighbor, it is only because we have enough other good food. But you do not have the same resources. It is definitely preferable to eat one's enemies than to leave the fruits of one's victory to the ravens and crows. But, gentlemen, surely you would not want to eat your friends. You think you will be roasting a Jesuit on a spit, but it is your defender, the enemy of your enemies, you are about to roast. As for me, I was born in your country. The gentleman you see before you is my master, and far from being a Jesuit, he has just killed one and is now wearing the spoils—hence your confusion. Should you wish to verify what I am saying, remove his cassock and take it to the nearest border of the Kingdom of Los Padres. There you can ask if my master has not killed a Jesuit officer. It won't take you long. You can still eat us afterward, if it turns out that I have lied to you. But if I have told you the truth, you know the principles of international jurisprudence, custom, and law only too well not to spare us."

The Orejones found this speech quite reasonable. They entrusted two dignitaries with the mission of hastening to find out the truth. The two delegates performed their task with elegance and soon returned with good news. The Orejones untied the two prisoners, treated them with much civility, offered them girls, served them refreshments, and brought them to the border of their land, exclaiming with joy, "He is definitely not a Jesuit! He is definitely not a Jesuit!"

Candide did not tire of marveling at the reason for his deliverance. "What a people!" he said. "What men! What customs! Had I not had the good fortune of driving my sword through the body of Mademoiselle Cunégonde's brother, I would have been eaten without fail. After all, the state of nature is good, for these people, instead of eating me, showed me a thousand courtesies the moment they realized I was not a Jesuit."

Chapter Seventeen

The arrival of Candide and his valet in the land of El Dorado, and what they saw there

When Candide and Cacambo arrived at the Orejones' border, Cacambo said, "As you see, this hemisphere is no better than the other. Believe me, we should return to Europe as fast as possible."

"How?" Candide asked. "And where should we go? If I go to my country, the Bulgars and the Avars will be butchering everyone; if I return to Portugal, I will be burned at the stake; if we stay in this country, we risk being roasted at any moment on a spit. But how can I bring myself to leave a part of the world where Mademoiselle Cunégonde is?"

"Let us head to Cayenne," Caçambo said. "We will find Frenchmen there who travel the whole world. They can help us. God will perhaps take pity on us."

It was not easy to travel to Cayenne. Candide and Cacambo knew more or less in which direction to go, but the mountains, rivers, precipices, brigands, and savages presented formidable obstacles. Their horses died of exhaustion. Their provisions ran out, and for a whole month they lived on wild fruit until they came upon a small river, along the banks of which grew coconut trees that sustained their lives and hopes.

Cacambo, who always gave as good advice as the old

woman, said to Candide, "We cannot go on like this. We have walked enough. I see an empty canoe on the riverbank. Let us fill it with coconuts and allow the current to carry us downstream. A river always leads to an inhabited place. If we don't find anything good, at least we will find something new."

"Let's go," Candide said. "We'll place ourselves in the hands of Providence."

They floated several leagues between banks that were at times covered with flowers, at times barren, at times flat, at times steep. The river grew wider and wider. Finally it disappeared beneath a vault of terrifying mountains that towered to the sky. The two travelers had the courage to abandon themselves to the waters beneath this vault, and the river, now narrower, drew them in with terrible speed and din. After twenty-four hours they saw daylight once more, but their canoe was smashed against some rocks, and they had to drag themselves from rock to rock for a whole league. At last they saw an immense horizon bordered by unscalable mountains, the land cultivated for both pleasure and need: everywhere, the useful was pleasant to look at. The roads were filled, or rather adorned, with splendidly shaped carriages made of a glittering material. These carriages carried men and women of singular beauty and were drawn by large red sheep that ran swifter than the finest horses of Andalusia, Tétouan, or Meknès.

"Now this is a land that is better than Westphalia!" Candide said.

They stopped at the first village they saw. Some children, covered in gold brocade that was torn and ragged, were playing quoits by the village gate. Our two men from the other world stopped to watch them. The disks they were throwing were quite large and round, yellow, red, and green, and shone with an unusual luster. The travelers were curious and picked up a few. They were made of gold, emeralds, and rubies, the smallest of which would have been the greatest ornament of the Mogul Throne.

"These children playing quoits are doubtless the sons of this country's king," Cacambo said.

The village schoolmaster appeared and called the children back to school.

"That must be the royal tutor," Candide said.

The little urchins immediately stopped playing and threw their disks and other toys on the ground. Candide picked them up and ran to the tutor, humbly presenting them to him, making him understand by signs that their Royal Highnesses had dropped their gold and precious stones. The village schoolmaster smiled and threw them away. He peered for an instant at Candide's face with great surprise, then went on his way.

The travelers did not fail to gather up the gold, rubies, and emeralds.

"Where are we?" Candide exclaimed. "The children of the kings of this country must be well brought up, as they are taught to look down on gold and precious stones."

Cacambo was as surprised as Candide. They came to the first house in the village. It was built like a European palace. A large crowd was bustling at the door, and there were even more people inside. Pleasant music and a delicious aroma of cooking filled the air. Cacambo approached the door and heard Peruvian being spoken. It was his mother tongue: as everyone knows, Cacambo was born in a village in Tucumán where nothing but this language was spoken.

"I shall be your interpreter," he told Candide. "This is an inn, let's go inside."

Two waiters and two waitresses, dressed in gold cloth,

their hair decorated with ribbons, immediately bade them sit at the table. They were served four soups, each garnished with two parrots, a boiled condor weighing two hundred pounds, two extremely delicious roasted monkeys, three hundred colibris on one platter and six hundred hummingbirds on another, exquisite stews, and delicious pastries. All this was served on dishes made of a kind of rock crystal. The waiters and waitresses poured an assortment of drinks made from sugarcane.

Their table companions were for the most part merchants and carters, all exceptionally polite, who asked Cacambo some questions with the most elegant discretion, and who answered his questions to his satisfaction.

When the meal was over, Cacambo thought—as did Candide—that he could pay the bill by throwing onto the table two of the large gold pieces he had picked up. The innkeeper and his wife burst out laughing, holding their sides for quite a while. Finally they regained their composure. "Gentlemen," the innkeeper said. "You are clearly not of these parts, though we are not accustomed to seeing foreigners. You must forgive us for laughing when you offer to pay for your meal with pebbles that you have picked up from our high roads. You probably do not have any of our country's currency, but you do not need any to dine here. All the inns are established for the convenience of commerce and are paid for by the government. The meal here was meager, because this is a poor village, but everywhere else you will be received as you deserve to be."

Cacambo explained the innkeeper's words to Candide, and Candide listened with the same admiration and astonishment with which his friend Cacambo reported them.

"What country can this be, unknown to the rest of the world, where nature is of a kind so different from ours?" they asked each other. "This must be the country where all is for the best, for there simply has to be such a country somewhere. Notwithstanding what Doctor Pangloss used to say, I often noticed that everything went badly in Westphalia."

Chapter Eighteen

What they saw in the land of El Dorado

Cacambo expressed all his wonderment to the innkeeper, who said to him, "I am extremely ignorant, and happy enough to be so. But we do have an old man in the village, retired from the royal court, who is the most learned man in the kingdom and the most eloquent."

He immediately took Cacambo to the old man's house. Candide, now relegated to a secondary role, accompanied his valet. They entered a very humble abode, for the door was only of silver, and the rooms paneled only in gold, but wrought with such taste that it eclipsed the most precious paneling. It is true the antechamber was merely inlaid with rubies and emeralds, but the way the furnishings were arranged made up for the room's extreme simplicity.

The old man received the two strangers on a sofa stuffed with hummingbird feathers and served them various liqueurs in diamond goblets. Then he satisfied their curiosity in the following terms: "I am a hundred and seventy-two years old, and my late father, equerry to the king, told me all about the astonishing revolutions in Peru that he had witnessed. The kingdom in which we are now is the old fatherland of the Incas who, leaving it very imprudently in order to subjugate another part of the world, were finally destroyed by the Spaniards.

"The princes and their families who stayed here in their

native land were wiser. With the consent of the people, they decreed that no inhabitant could ever leave this little kingdom, and this is what has conserved our innocence and happiness. The Spaniards had only the vaguest knowledge of our country—they named it El Dorado—and an Englishman by the name of Sir Raleigh almost reached our kingdom about a hundred years ago; but as we are encircled by impassable mountains and precipices, we have always been sheltered from the greed of the European nations, who have a boundless passion for our pebbles and mud, and who would kill each and every one of us to lay their hands on them."

The conversation was long. It touched on the form of government, the customs, women, public spectacles, and the arts. Finally Candide, who always had a taste for metaphysics, had Cacambo ask if this country had a religion.

The old man's cheeks flushed. "What! How can you doubt it?" he said. "Do you take us for ingrates?"

Cacambo humbly asked what the religion of El Dorado was.

The old man colored once more. "Can there be two religions?" he said. "We have, I believe, the same religion as everyone else in the world: we worship God from dusk to dawn."

"You worship only one God?" Cacambo asked, still serving as the interpreter of Candide's doubts.

"Obviously," the old man said. "As there are neither two, nor three, nor four. I must say that the people of your world ask the strangest things."

Candide did not tire of putting questions to the old man. He wanted to know how people prayed to God in El Dorado.

"We don't pray at all," the good, respectable sage replied.

"We have nothing to ask of Him. He has given us everything we need, and we thank him incessantly."

Candide was curious to meet some priests. He had Cacambo ask where they might find some.

The old man smiled. "My friends," he said, "we are all priests here. The king and the heads of all the households gather to sing solemn hymns of thanksgiving every morning, accompanied by five or six thousand musicians."

"What? You don't have monks who preach, argue, govern, plot, and have people burned who do not share their opinions?"

"We would have to be mad," the old man replied. "We are all of the same opinion here and have no idea what you mean by those monks of yours."

Candide was in ecstasy throughout the conversation. "This is quite different from Westphalia and the castle of His Lordship the Baron," he said to himself. "If our friend Pangloss had seen El Dorado, he would not have said that the castle of Thunder-Ten-Tronckh was the best place in the world. One definitely must travel."

After this long conversation, the good old man had a carriage harnessed with six sheep and gave twelve of his servants to the two travelers to escort them to the royal court.

"You must excuse me," he said. "My age deprives me of the honor of accompanying you. The king will receive you in a manner which will not displease you, and you will doubtless pardon the customs of the land if some of them affront you."

Candide and Cacambo climbed into the carriage. The six sheep flew off, and in less than four hours they arrived at the king's palace, which was situated at one end of the capital. The portal was two hundred and twenty feet high and a hundred feet wide. It is impossible to describe what it was made of, but it is easy enough to imagine the superiority it had over all the pebbles and sand we call gold or gems.

Twenty beautiful girls of the guard received Candide and Cacambo as they stepped out of the carriage. They led them to the baths and dressed them in robes of a cloth made of the down of hummingbirds. After this, the grand masters and grand ladies of the crown escorted them, as was the custom, between two rows of a thousand musicians each to the chamber of His Majesty. As they approached the throne room, Cacambo asked one of the grand masters how one should comport oneself in greeting His Majesty. Did one fall to one's knees or prostrate oneself, did one place one's hands on one's head or one's bottom, or did one lick the dust off the floor? In a word, what was the custom?

"Our custom," the grand master replied, "is to hug the king and give him a kiss on both cheeks."

Candide and Cacambo threw their arms around His Majesty, who received them with all the charm imaginable and politely asked them to dinner that evening. In the meantime they were shown the city, with public buildings that rose to the clouds, market arcades adorned with a thousand columns, fountains of pure water, fountains of rose water, and fountains of sugarcane juice that flowed continually in the town squares, which were paved with gems redolent of cloves and cinnamon. Candide asked to see the law court. He was told that there was no such thing, and that no one ever litigated. He asked if there were any prisons and was told that there were none. What surprised him even more and gave him the most pleasure was the palace of sciences, in which he saw a gallery two thousand paces long filled with instruments of mathematics and physics.

After having toured only a thousandth part of the city during the entire afternoon, they were taken back to the palace. Candide sat down to table with the king, Cacambo, and several ladies. Never had they feasted so sumptuously, nor had there ever been wittier conversation than that of His Majesty. Cacambo explained the king's remarks to Candide, which even in translation lost none of their wit. This was not the least of all the things that astonished Candide.

They spent a month in this sanctuary. "It is true, my friend," Candide did not tire of telling Cacambo, "I will say this yet again: the castle in which I was born does not compare with this land we are in. But Mademoiselle Cunégonde is not here, and you no doubt have a mistress in Europe. If we stay here, we will only be like the others. Yet if we return to our world with just twelve sheep laden with El Dorado pebbles, we will be wealthier than all the kings put together. We will not need to fear inquisitors ever again and will easily win back Mademoiselle Cunégonde."

Cacambo liked these words. A man does love to travel, to be admired back home, and to boast about what he has seen on his voyages—so the two fortunate men decided to stop being fortunate and ask His Majesty's permission to leave.

"You are doing a foolish thing," the king told them. "I am aware that my country does not amount to much, but if one is comfortable in a place, one ought to stay there. Yet I surely do not have the right to make foreigners stay: that would be an act of tyranny not supported by our customs or our laws. All men are free. You may leave whenever you like, but the way out is difficult. It is impossible to go back up the fast-flowing river by which you miraculously arrived and which flows beneath the vault of rocks. The mountains that surround my kingdom are ten thousand feet high and tower like walls. Each mountain covers a space of more than ten leagues. One can only descend by way of precipices. Since you absolutely wish to leave, however, I will order my engineers to build a machine that can transport you in comfort. But after you have been brought to the other side of the mountains, nobody will be able to accompany you, as my subjects have taken an oath never to leave this refuge, and they are too wise to break their vow. You may ask me for anything else you want."

"All we ask of Your Majesty," Cacambo said, "is a few sheep laden with provisions, pebbles, and some of the mud of your country."

The king laughed. "I cannot understand the taste you Europeans have for our yellow mud," he said. "But you can take as much as you like, and a lot of good may it do you."

He immediately ordered his engineers to build a machine that would hoist the two extraordinary men out of the kingdom. Three thousand excellent engineers worked on it, and it was ready in two weeks, not costing more than twenty million pounds sterling in the local currency. Candide and Cacambo were placed in the machine, as were two large red sheep with saddles and bridles that would serve them as mounts on the other side of the mountains, twenty pack sheep laden with provisions, thirty that carried gifts of the strangest articles the country had to offer, and fifty laden with gold, gems, and diamonds. The king tenderly embraced the two vagabonds.

Their departure made a fine spectacle, as did the ingenious manner in which they and their sheep were raised over the mountains. The engineers, after they brought them to safety, took their leave, and Candide's only remaining desire was to present his sheep to Mademoiselle Cunégonde.

"We are now wealthy enough to pay the Governor of

Buenos Aires," he said. "That is, if a price can be set on Mademoiselle Cunégonde. Let us go to Cayenne, take a ship, and then we can give some thought to which kingdom we might want to buy."

Chapter Nineteen

What happened to them in Surinam, and how Candide met Martin

Our two travelers' first day was quite pleasant. They were sustained by the thought of seeing themselves possessors of more treasure than could be gathered in all of Asia, Europe, and Africa. Candide was elated and carved Cunégonde's name on tree trunks. On the second day, two of their sheep fell into a swamp and were swallowed up with their loads. A few days later two more sheep died of exhaustion. Seven or eight perished of hunger in a desert. Then some others fell down a precipice. Finally, after a hundred days of travel, they had only two sheep left.

"My friend," Candide said, "you see how perishable the riches of this world are. Nothing can endure but virtue and the happiness of seeing Mademoiselle Cunégonde again."

"I agree," Cacambo replied. "But we still have two sheep left, carrying more treasure than the King of Spain will ever own, and I can see in the distance a town that I imagine must be Surinam, which belongs to the Dutch. We are at the end of our troubles and at the beginning of our happiness."

As they approached the town, they came across a Negro lying on the ground with only half his clothes on. That is, nothing but a pair of blue underpants. The poor man's left leg and right hand were missing.

"My God!" Candide said to him in Dutch. "What are

you doing here in the terrible condition I see you in, my friend?"

"I am waiting for my master, Monsieur Vanderdendur, the famous merchant," the Negro replied.*

"Is it Monsieur Vanderdendur who has done this to you?" Candide asked.

"Yes, sir," the Negro replied. "It is the custom. For clothing we are only given a pair of underpants twice a year. When we work in the sugar mills and one of our fingers is caught in the gears, they cut off our hand. When we try to escape, we get a leg cut off. I found myself in both situations. This is the price for which you eat sugar in Europe. And yet when my mother sold me for ten Spanish patagon crowns on the coast of Guinea, she told me, 'My dear child, always revere our witch doctors, you must always worship them, they will make you live happily. You have the honor of being a slave of the whites, our masters, and in this way you have made your mother's and father's fortune.' Alas, I do not know if I did make their fortune, but they haven't made mine. Dogs, monkeys, and parrots are a thousand times less unfortunate than we are. The Dutch witch doctors who converted me tell me every Sunday in church that we are all, whites and blacks, children of Adam. I am not a genealogist, but if what these preachers say is true, then we are all first cousins. You will have to admit that one cannot treat relatives in a more terrible manner than this."

"O Pangloss!" Candide exclaimed. "You had not supposed that such an abomination was possible! That's it! I finally must renounce your Optimism!"

"What is Optimism?" Cacambo asked.

"Alas!" Candide replied. "It is the mania of affirming

* This is a possible reference to Van Duren, a Dutch publisher, whom Voltaire called "the most eminent rogue of his kind."

that everything is good when things are bad." Looking at the Negro, he wept and, weeping, entered Surinam.

The first thing they asked was whether there was a vessel in the port that could be sent to Buenos Aires. The man they spoke to happened to be a Spanish captain, who offered to strike an honest bargain and arranged to meet them later at a tavern. Candide and the faithful Cacambo went to wait for him there with their two sheep.

Candide, who always wore his heart on his sleeve, told the Spaniard all his adventures and vouched to rescue Mademoiselle Cunégonde.

"I would not be foolish enough to take you to Buenos Aires," the captain said. "I would be hanged, and you would be too. The fair Cunégonde is the governor's favorite mistress."

This was a terrible blow to Candide. He wept for a long time. Finally he took Cacambo aside. "This is what you have to do, my dear friend," Candide said. "Each of us has diamonds in our pockets worth five or six million. You are cleverer than I am. Go rescue Mademoiselle Cunégonde from Buenos Aires. If the governor proves difficult, give him a million. If he does not yield, give him two. You haven't killed an inquisitor, no one will mistrust you. I will fit out another ship and go to Venice, where I shall wait for you. It is a free nation in which we need fear neither Bulgars, Avars, Jews, nor inquisitors."

Cacambo applauded this wise decision. He was in despair at having to part with such a good master, who had become his intimate friend. But the pleasure of being of service to Candide overcame the pain of leaving him. They embraced and wept. Candide urged him not to forget the worthy old woman. Cacambo set out that very day. He was a fine fellow indeed!

Candide stayed awhile longer in Surinam, waiting for a

captain to take him and his two remaining sheep to Italy. He hired servants and bought everything he would need for the long voyage. Finally Monsieur Vanderdendur, who owned a large ship, came to introduce himself.

"How much do you want in order to take me, my servants, my baggage, and these sheep straight to Venice?" Candide asked him.

The shipowner offered to take him for ten thousand piastres, and Candide agreed without hesitation.

"Aha!" the sensible Vanderdendur said to himself. "This foreigner is giving me ten thousand piastres just like that. He must be very rich." Then, returning a few moments later, he said he could not take him for less than twenty thousand.

"Fine, you shall have them," Candide replied.

"Well!" the merchant mumbled. "This man is as ready to pay twenty thousand as he was to pay ten!" He returned again and said he could not take him to Venice for less than thirty thousand piastres.

"So I will pay you thirty thousand," Candide said.

"Aha!" the Dutch merchant thought. "Thirty thousand piastres are nothing to this man. Those two sheep must be carrying immense treasures. Let's not insist any further. Let him pay the thirty thousand, and then we'll see."

Candide sold two small diamonds, the lesser of which was worth more than all the money the shipowner was asking. He paid in advance. The sheep were put onboard, and Candide followed in a small boat to join the ship out in the harbor. The Dutchman seized the opportunity, hoisted sail, and set off. The wind favored him. Candide, astounded and frantic, soon lost sight of him.

"Alas!" he cried. "Here's a trick worthy of the old world!"

He returned to shore, overwhelmed with grief, for he

had lost the means with which to make a fortune worth that of twenty monarchs.

He made his way to the house of the Dutch judge and, as he was somewhat perturbed, began knocking roughly on the door. He went inside and told his tale, shouting a little more loudly than was proper. The judge began by fining him ten thousand piastres for the noise he had made. Then he listened to him patiently, promised to examine the matter as soon as the Dutchman returned, and had Candide pay him another ten thousand piastres for the expenses of the consultation.

These developments cast Candide into utter despair. It is true that he had endured misfortunes a thousand times more painful, but the cold-bloodedness of the judge and of the Dutch merchant who had robbed him inflamed his bile and plunged him into black melancholy. He saw before him the wickedness of men in all its ugliness; he was filled with gloomy thoughts. But there was a French ship in the harbor that was on the point of leaving for Bordeaux. As Candide no longer had sheep laden with diamonds to bring onboard, he booked a cabin at the right price and had it announced in town that he would pay the passage, food, and two thousand piastres to an honest man who would undertake the journey with him, provided that the man was the most unfortunate person in all the province and the most disgusted with his condition.

Such a large crowd of claimants presented themselves that a whole fleet could not have carried them. Candide, wishing to narrow down his choice, picked some twenty men who seemed quite companionable, all of whom claimed that they deserved to be chosen. He assembled them at his inn and gave them supper, on condition that each would swear to tell his story faithfully. He promised to choose the one who seemed most deserving of pity and who had the most reason to be discontented with his lot. The others wouldn't leave empty-handed.

The meeting lasted until four in the morning. Candide, hearing all their tales, remembered what the old woman had said during the voyage to Buenos Aires and the wager she had made, that there was not a single person on the ship who had not endured great misfortunes. With every story he was told, he thought of Pangloss. "Pangloss would be quite hard put to prove his system," he said to himself. "I wish he were here. Certainly, if all is well, it is in El Dorado and not in the rest of the world."

Finally Candide decided in favor of a poor scholar who had worked for ten years for the publishers of Amsterdam. Candide judged that there was no more disgusting profession in the world.*

This scholar, who was also a good man, had been robbed by his wife, beaten by his son, and abandoned by his daughter, who arranged for a Portuguese to abduct her. He had just been dismissed from a minor post that barely sustained him, and the preachers of Surinam were persecuting him because they took him for a Socinian.† It is true that the others were at least as unfortunate as this scholar was, but Candide was hoping he would entertain him during the voyage. All the scholar's rivals felt that Candide was doing them a great injustice, but he appeased them by giving them each a hundred piastres.

* Amsterdam was a major center for publishing in the eighteenth century. Voltaire had difficult dealings with Dutch publishers, particularly with Van Duren, who Voltaire felt had cheated him on a book that Frederick the Great had written and Voltaire had edited.

† A member of an Antitrinitarian sect founded in the sixteenth century by Laelius Socinus and his nephew Faustus Socinus. The Socinians clashed with the Catholic Church as they denied the doctrines of Original Sin, Hell, and Christ's divinity.

Chapter Twenty

What happened to Candide and Martin at sea

So Candide and the old scholar, whose name was Martin, set out for Bordeaux. Both had seen much and suffered much. If the ship were to have sailed all the way from Surinam to Japan by way of the Cape of Good Hope, they would not have lacked for conversation about moral evil and physical evil.

Candide, however, did have a great advantage over Martin: he still hoped to see Mademoiselle Cunégonde again, while Martin had nothing to hope for. Furthermore, Candide did have some gold and diamonds. Though he had lost a hundred big red sheep loaded with the earth's greatest treasures, and though the Dutch merchant's mischief still pained him, when he thought of what remained in his pockets and when he spoke of Cunégonde, especially at the end of a meal, he once more inclined toward Pangloss's philosophy.

"As for you, Monsieur Martin," he said to the scholar, "what do you think of all that? What is your opinion on moral evil and physical evil?"

"Monsieur," Martin replied, "my priests have accused me of being a Socinian. But to tell the truth, I am a Manichaean."*

"You are making fun of me," Candide said. "There are no Manichaeans left in the world."

* Manichaeans believed in pure reason as opposed to Christian belief in faith. Manichaeanism taught that life in this world is unbearably painful and radically evil, and that knowledge is the only way to salvation. It was a dualistic religion, presenting God and Satan as coeternal.

"There is me," Martin replied. "I don't know what to do, but I cannot think differently."

"You must be possessed by the Devil," Candide said.

"He meddles so much in the affairs of this world that he might well be inside me, just as he is everywhere," Martin said. "But I confess that as I cast my eye over this globe, or rather this globule, I think that God has abandoned it to some evil being. I except El Dorado, of course. I have hardly ever come across a town that does not desire the ruin of its neighboring town, a family that does not desire to destroy another family. Everywhere the weak despise the strong at whose feet they grovel, and the strong treat them like sheep whose wool and flesh can be sold. A million regimented assassins, marching from one end of Europe to the other, perform disciplined murder and robbery to earn their bread, because no profession is more honest. In cities where peace and the arts flourish, men are more consumed by jealousy, worry, and anxiety than they are in cities under the blight of a besieging army. Private sorrows are more bitter than public suffering. In a word, I have seen and suffered so much that I am a Manichaean."

"There is some good in this," Candide said.

"That may be," Martin replied. "But I do not know what it is."

In the midst of this discussion, a cannon shot was heard. From moment to moment the din grew louder. Each took up his spyglass. They saw two ships engaged in battle about three miles away. The wind brought both ships so close to the French vessel that they had the pleasure of viewing the battle at their ease. Finally, one ship fired a salvo so low and well aimed that it sank the other. Candide and Martin distinctly saw a hundred or so men on the deck of the sinking ship. They had all raised their hands to Heaven, uttering horrifying cries. An instant later, they were swallowed up.

"There you have it," Martin said. "This is how men treat one another."

"It is true that it is rather diabolical," Candide said. As he spoke, he noticed something bright red swimming toward their ship. A boat was sent out to see what it might be. It was one of Candide's sheep. Candide was happier at finding this sheep again than he had been sorry at losing a hundred of them laden with large El Dorado diamonds.

The French captain ascertained that the captain of the victorious ship was a Spaniard, and that the captain of the ship that had been sunk was a Dutch pirate—the very same who had robbed Candide. The immense riches that the blackguard had seized had now sunk with him to the bottom of the ocean, and only one sheep was saved.

"As you see," Candide said to Martin, "crime is sometimes punished. This rascal of a Dutch captain got the fate he deserved."

"I agree," Martin replied. "But did the passengers on his ship have to perish too? God punished that scoundrel, but the Devil drowned the others."

Meanwhile, the French and Spanish ships went their separate ways, and Candide continued his discussions with Martin. They debated for two weeks without respite, though at the end of that time they had got no further than they had been on the first day. But at least they were talking, expressing their ideas, and consoling each other. Candide caressed his sheep.

"Since I have found you again," he said, "I am sure I can also find Cunégonde."

Chapter Twenty-one

Candide and Martin continue reasoning as they approach the coast of France

The coast of France finally came into view.

"Have you ever been to France, Monsieur Martin?" Candide asked.

"Yes," Martin replied, "I have traveled through several provinces. In some, half the people are mad, in others the people are too cunning; there are some in which they are gentle and foolish, and others again where everyone is witty. And in all these provinces the main occupation is love, the second slander, and the third talking nonsense."

"But, Monsieur Martin, have you ever seen Paris?"

"Yes, I have seen Paris. It has all those types of people. What chaos! A swarm of people where everyone is seeking pleasure but hardly anyone finds it; at least that is how it seemed to me. I did not stay long. When I arrived, pickpockets at the Saint-Germain fair robbed me of everything I had. Then I was mistaken for a thief and spent a week in jail, after which I worked as a proofreader in order to earn enough to return to Holland on foot. I came to know the writing rabble, the plotting rabble, and the convulsionary rabble.* They say there are some very refined people in that city, and I would like to believe it."

"As for me, I have no interest in seeing France," Candide said. "As I am sure you realize, when one has spent a month in El Dorado one no longer cares to see anything on earth

* The convulsionists gathered at the grave of François Pâris, a Jansenist divine who died in 1727. They fell to the ground in convulsions, eating dirt off the grave site, and participated in ritual beatings and crucifixions.

but Mademoiselle Cunégonde. I will go and wait for her in Venice. We must cross France to reach Italy. Would you like to accompany me?"

"Gladly," Martin replied. "They say that Venice is only good for noble Venetians but that they welcome foreigners who have a lot of money. I don't have any, but you do. I will follow you anywhere."

"By the way," Candide said, "do you believe that the world was originally a sea, as that big book the ship captain had claims?"*

"I don't believe it at all," Martin replied. "I don't believe any of those fantasies they've been fobbing off on us for some time now."

"But then what was this world created for?" Candide asked.

"To infuriate us," Martin replied.

"Were you not astonished by the love that the two girls of the land of the Orejones had for those monkeys I told you about?" Candide continued.

"Not at all," Martin said. "I do not see what is so strange about that sort of passion. I have seen so many extraordinary things that nothing is extraordinary anymore."

"Do you believe that men always butchered one another the way they do today?" Candide asked. "Do you believe they have always been liars, rogues, traitors, ingrates, brigands, weaklings, inconstant, cowards, enviers, gluttons, drunkards, misers, self-seekers, bloodthirsty, slanderers, debauchees, fanatics, hypocrites, and fools?"

"Do you believe that hawks have always eaten pigeons wherever they have found them?" Martin asked.

* Books such as *Théorie de la terre* (1749) by Georges Buffon and *Histoires des navigations aux terres australes* (1756) by Charles de Brosses popularized scientific theories suggesting that the world had begun as an ocean.

"Yes, definitely," Candide replied.

"Very well," Martin said. "If hawks have always had the same character, why would you expect men to have changed theirs?"

"Oh, but there is quite a difference," Candide said, "for, after all, free will . . ."

Reasoning in this way, they arrived at Bordeaux.

Chapter Twenty-two

What happened to Candide and Martin in France

Candide stopped in Bordeaux only long enough to sell a few El Dorado pebbles and acquire a fine chaise for two, as he could no longer do without his philosopher, Martin. He was vexed at having to part with his sheep, which he left to the Academy of Sciences at Bordeaux. For its annual prize, the Academy proposed a study that would elucidate why the wool of this sheep was red. The prize was awarded to a scholar from the north, who proved by way of *a* plus *b* minus *c* divided by *z* that the sheep had to be red and would die of sheep pox.

Meanwhile, all the travelers Candide met at roadside inns told him that they were on their way to Paris. This eagerness for Paris finally roused Candide's desire to see the capital. It was easy enough to change direction from the road to Venice. He entered Paris by the Faubourg Saint-Marceau and thought himself in the nastiest little village in Westphalia.*

Candide was scarcely settled in his inn when he was

* The Faubourg Saint-Marceau was at the time one of the disreputable parts of Paris.

beset by a slight illness brought on by exhaustion. As an enormous diamond was spotted on his finger, and a prodigiously heavy box in his carriage, he immediately found at his side two doctors he had not summoned, several intimate friends who would not leave him, and two pious women who heated up soups for him.

"I remember falling sick in Paris too, during my first voyage," Martin said. "I was very poor, and so had neither friends, nor doctors, nor pious women cooking for me. And yet I still recovered."

Meanwhile, by dint of the medicines and bloodlettings, Candide's illness became serious. A local deacon came to ask him sweetly for a note payable to the bearer for the next world.* Candide refused to comply. The pious women assured him that this was the new fashion. Candide replied that he was not a man of fashion. Martin wanted to throw the deacon out the window, and the cleric swore that Candide would not be buried. Martin swore that he would bury the cleric if he continued importuning them. The quarrel became heated. Martin grabbed him by the shoulders and pushed him out the door, which caused a great scandal and led to court proceedings.

Candide began to recover and during his convalescence had very good company at the dinner table. They gambled for high stakes. Candide was quite astonished that he never got the aces, but Martin was not.

Among the people who did him the honors of the town was a small abbé from Périgord, one of those attentive men who are always alert, obliging, shameless, fawning, and accommodating, who lie in wait for travelers, telling them

* Voltaire is punning on "banknote" as opposed to a dying person's "note of confession," which had to be witnessed by a Catholic priest to ensure burial in consecrated earth.

scandalous tales of the city and offering them every pleasure at a price. First the abbé took Martin and Candide to the theater, where a new tragedy was being performed. Candide found himself seated next to some great wits, which did not stop him from being moved to tears by some scenes that were beautifully performed. During the intermission, one of the wits sitting next to him said, "You are quite wrong to cry. The actress is very bad, the actor playing with her is even worse, and the play is even worse than the actors. The playwright does not know a word of Arabic, and yet the play is set in Arabia.* Furthermore, he is a man who does not believe in innate ideas. Tomorrow I will bring you twenty pamphlets attacking him."

"Monsieur, how many plays do you have in France?" Candide asked the abbé.

"Five or six thousand," the latter replied.

"That is a great number," Candide said. "How many good ones are there among them?"

"Fifteen or sixteen," the abbé replied.

"That is a great number," Martin said.

Candide was very impressed by an actress who played Queen Elizabeth in a rather flat tragedy that was performed from time to time.†

"I like this actress very much," he told Martin. "There is something about her that reminds me of Cunégonde. I would like to pay her my respects."

The abbé from Périgord offered to introduce him. Candide, who had been brought up in Germany, asked what the etiquette was, and how the queens of England should be approached in France.

* This might be a humorous reference to Voltaire's own play *Le fanatisme, ou Mahomet le prophète,* first performed in 1741.

† A reference to the play *Le comte d'Essex* by Thomas Corneille.

"One must make a distinction," the abbé replied. "In the provinces one takes them to an inn; in Paris one shows them respect while they are beautiful but throws them onto a garbage dump when they are dead."*

"Queens on a garbage dump?" Candide exclaimed.

"Yes," Martin replied. "The abbé is right. I was in Paris when Mademoiselle Monime passed, as the saying goes, from this life to the next, and she was refused what the clergy call 'the honor of burial,' in other words the honor of rotting with all the beggars of the neighborhood in a squalid cemetery.† She was the only one in her troupe to be buried at the corner of the rue de Bourgogne, which would have upset her greatly, as she had a noble mind."‡

"That was very unkind," Candide said.

"What do you expect?" Martin replied. "That's how these people are. Imagine all the contradictions, all the possible incompatibilities: you see them in the government, in the courts, in the churches, and on the stages of this mad country."

"Is it true that people in Paris are always laughing?" Candide asked.

"Yes," the abbé replied, "but it is angry laughter. They complain about everything with peals of laughter. They even commit the most detestable actions while laughing."

"Who was that fat pig who was telling me so many bad things about the play that made me weep so much, and in

* Actors and actresses were automatically excommunicated, and so refused burial in consecrated earth.

† Adrienne Lecouvreur, 1692–1730, one of the foremost actresses of her time, was an intimate friend of Voltaire. One of her most celebrated roles was Monime in Racine's play *Mithridate.* When she died unexpectedly, she was refused burial in consecrated earth. Voltaire campaigned against this practice.

‡ After Adrienne Lecouvreur's body was refused burial by the church, the police ordered it to be buried in a lime pit near the rue de Bourgogne and rue de Grenelle by the banks of the Seine.

which the actors gave me so much pleasure?" Candide asked.

"He is poison incarnate," the abbé replied. "He makes a living by saying bad things about every play and every book. He hates anyone who is successful the way a eunuch hates a sensualist. He is one of those serpents of literature who feed on mud and venom. He is a foliator."

"What do you mean by foliator?" Candide asked.

"Someone who writes folios," the abbé said, "a Fréron."*

This was how Candide, Martin, and the abbé from Périgord reasoned on the steps of the theater as they watched the crowd filing out of the foyer.

"Though I am most anxious to see Mademoiselle Cunégonde again," Candide said, "I would still like to dine with Mademoiselle Clairon, for she seems quite admirable."†

The abbé was not a man to approach Mademoiselle Clairon, who only frequented good society. "She is engaged this evening," he told Candide, "but I could bring you to a lady of quality at whose salon you will get to know Paris as if you had lived here for four years."

Candide, curious by nature, asked to be taken to this lady at the far end of the Faubourg St.-Honoré.‡ The company there was playing faro. Twelve sad punters each held a hand of cards—earmarked records of their misfortune.§

* Élie-Catherine Fréron, 1719–1776, known in his time as "The Illustrious Fréron," was a prominent critic and founder of the influential magazine *L'Année littéraire*. He was one of Voltaire's most vocal and vitriolic opponents.

† La Clairon, 1723–1803, one of the leading actresses of the Comédie-Française, was renowned for her interpretation of roles in Voltaire's plays.

‡ The Faubourg St.-Honoré was one of the most elegant neighborhoods of Paris in the eighteenth century.

§ Faro was a card game popular in the eighteenth century in which a number of players, "punters," played against a "banker," setting stakes on their cards, which

Profound silence reigned. There was a pallor on the punters' brows, and anxiety on the banker's. The lady of the house, seated next to the pitiless banker, caught with her lynx's eyes every illicit *paroli* or *sept-et-le-va* with which players might earmark their cards. She had them straighten out the corners with severe but polite firmness, without any sign of anger, as she did not want to lose her regulars.* The lady called herself the Marquise de Parolignac.† Her fifteen-year-old daughter sat among the punters, forewarning her mother with a wink of any attempt that these poor men might make to counter the cruelty of fortune. The abbé from Périgord, Candide, and Martin entered the room. Nobody rose, greeted, or glanced up at them. Everyone was deeply absorbed in the game.

"Baroness Thunder-Ten-Tronckh was more polite," Candide said.

Meanwhile, the abbé leaned down to the marquise's ear. She half rose, honoring Candide with a graceful smile and Martin with a nod that was very noble indeed. She called for a chair and cards for Candide, and he lost fifty thousand francs in two rounds, after which the party dined cheerfully. Everyone was quite astonished that Candide was not distressed by his loss. "He must be an English milord," the lackeys whispered among themselves in their lackey slang.

The dinner was like most Parisian dinners: first there was

---

they earmarked. Hence, after they lost, their earmarked cards were "records of their misfortune."

* *Paroli* is a doubling of the stakes, and *sept-et-le-va* is multiplying the stakes by seven. A way of cheating at faro would be to try earmarking cards once the game is under way and it is clear on which cards the stakes ought to have been placed.

† The name Marquise de Parolignac is fabricated from the card term *paroli.*

silence, then a din of indistinguishable words, followed by banter filled for the most part with insipid and bogus news, false reasoning, a little politics, and much bad-mouthing. They even spoke of new books.

"Have you seen the novel by that fellow Gauchat, Doctor of Theology?" the abbé inquired of the company.*

"Yes," one of the guests replied. "But I could not finish it. There is a mountain of outrageous things being published right now, though it is true that everything put together does not match the outrageousness of Gauchat, Doctor of Theology. I am so tired of the immense quantity of these detestable books that are inundating us that I have given myself over to playing faro."

"What about the miscellanies of Archdeacon T., what do you think of those?" the abbé asked.†

"Ah," Madame de Parolignac exclaimed, "what a terrible bore the archdeacon is! How curiously he tells us everything the whole world already knows. How ponderously he talks about matters that are not even worth mentioning casually! How witlessly he appropriates the wit of others! How he spoils all he pillages! How he disgusts me! But he will disgust me no more: it is enough to have read a few pages the archdeacon has penned."

A man of learning and taste who was sitting at the table seconded the marquise's words. The talk turned to tragedies. The marquise asked why there were tragedies that might be performed but could not be read. The man of taste ex-

* Gabriel Gauchat, 1709–1774, was a man of the church and literary figure. He was a vocal opponent of the philosophers, attacking their work from a Catholic viewpoint.

† Nicolas Trublet, 1697–1770, was a man of the church, literary figure, and member of the Académie Française. Voltaire had been an admirer of his works until Trublet wrote: "In the *Henriade* [an epic of Voltaire's] it is not the poet who bores one and makes one yawn: it is the poetry, or rather the verse."

plained that a play could be of some interest and yet still have barely any merit. He demonstrated in a few words that it was not enough to convey one or two situations that could be found in any novel, which would invariably win over the spectators, but that a playwright had to be innovative without being bizarre, that he had to be often sublime and always natural. A playwright had to know the human heart and make it speak, and be a great poet without any of the characters in the play coming across as poets themselves. A playwright had to know his language perfectly and speak it with purity and uninterrupted harmony, the rhyme never detracting from the meaning.

"Whoever does not observe these rules," he added, "might pen one or two tragedies that will be applauded in the theaters but will never be counted among the fine writers. There are very few good tragedies. Some are idylls in dialogue, well written and well rhymed, others are political arguments that put you to sleep, or revolting exaggerations. Still others are the dreams of maniacs in barbarous style, incoherent speeches, long apostrophes to the gods because the writer does not know how to speak to people, false maxims, and pompous platitudes."

Candide listened to these words attentively and formed a high opinion of the speaker. As the marquise had taken care to seat Candide next to her, he leaned over to her ear and took the liberty of inquiring who the man who spoke so well might be.

"He is a scholar who never plays cards," the lady said. "The abbé sometimes brings him to dine. He is an expert in tragedies and books, and has written a tragedy that was hissed out of the theater and a book that has never been seen outside his bookseller's shop, except for a signed copy he gave me."

"What a great man!" Candide exclaimed. "He is another

Pangloss!" And, turning to the scholar, he said, "Monsieur, you doubtless believe that everything is for the best in the physical and moral worlds, and that nothing could be otherwise."

"Me, sir? I do not believe that at all," the scholar replied. "I think that everything tends to go wrong in our world. No one knows his place or his duty, no one knows what he does or ought to do, and except for dinners, which are quite cheerful and where there seems to be some congeniality, all the rest of one's time is passed in surly quarreling: Jansenists against Molinists, men of the parliament against men of the church, men of letters against men of letters, courtesans against courtesans, financiers against the people, wives against husbands, and relatives against relatives.* It is an eternal war."

"I have seen worse," Candide replied. "But a sage who had the misfortune of being hanged taught me that it is all wonderful, the shadows of a beautiful painting."

"Your hanged man was making fun of the world!" Martin said. "Those shadows are terrible stains!"

"It is men who make stains," Candide replied. "And they cannot avoid it."

"So it is not their fault," Martin said.

Most of the punters, who understood nothing of this talk, were drinking. Martin debated with the scholar, and Candide recounted to the lady of the house some of his adventures.

After dinner, the marquise led Candide to her boudoir and invited him to sit on a sofa.

* A Jansenist was a follower of the doctrines of Cornelis Jansen, 1585–1638, who considered natural human will perverse and believed that, without divine help, a human being could not be saved. A Molinist was a follower of the doctrines of the Spanish Jesuit theologian Luis de Molina, 1535–1600, and an opponent of Jansenism.

"So," she said, "am I to understand that you are still desperately in love with Mademoiselle Cunégonde de Thunder-Ten-Tronckh?"

"Yes, Madame," Candide replied.

"You speak like a young Westphalian," the marquise said with a tender smile. "A Frenchman would have said: 'It is true that I did once love Mademoiselle Cunégonde, but the moment I saw you, Madame, I fear I love her no longer.' "

"Alas, Madame," said Candide, "I will reply as you wish."

"Your passion for her began when you picked up her handkerchief," the marquise said. "I want you to pick up my garter."

"With all my heart," Candide replied and picked it up.

"But I want you to put it back where it belongs," the lady said, and Candide did so. "You see," she continued, "you are a foreigner. I sometimes make my Parisian lovers languish for two whole weeks, but I am offering myself to you on our first night, because one has to bestow the honors of one's country on a young man from Westphalia."

The beautiful woman, having noticed two enormous diamonds on the young foreigner's hands, praised them with such exuberance that they passed from Candide's fingers to those of the marquise.

As Candide left with the abbé from Périgord, he felt some remorse at having been unfaithful to Mademoiselle Cunégonde. The abbé was very sympathetic. He had secured only a small share of the fifty thousand pounds that Candide had lost at the card table, and a passing share of the value of the two diamonds that had been half given, half extorted. His intent was to profit as much as possible from the advantages that his acquaintance with Candide would bring him. The abbé spoke to him a good deal about

Cunégonde, and Candide told him that he would certainly beg that beauty's forgiveness when he saw her in Venice.

The abbé redoubled his courtesy and attentions, and took a tender interest in everything that Candide said, did, and wanted to do.

"So, Monsieur," the abbé said, "you have a rendezvous in Venice?"

"Yes," Candide replied, "I absolutely must find Mademoiselle Cunégonde." And elated by the pleasure of speaking about the object of his love, he recounted, as was his custom, some of his adventures with that illustrious Westphalian beauty.

"Am I right in assuming that Mademoiselle Cunégonde has a fine wit and writes charming letters?" the abbé asked.

"I have never received any," Candide replied. "For, you see, as I was chased from the castle because of my love for her, I could not write to her. And then I heard that she was dead, and then found her again, lost her again, and then sent a messenger to her, two thousand five hundred leagues from here. I am awaiting a reply."

The abbé was listening attentively, though his thoughts seemed elsewhere. He soon took leave of the two foreigners with tender embraces. The next morning, on awakening, Candide received a letter composed in the following terms:

Dear Monsieur, Dearest Love,

It is a week now that I have been ill in this city. I have heard that you are here. I would fly to your arms were I able to move. In Bordeaux I heard that you were here. I left faithful Cacambo and the old woman there, and they are to follow me soon. The Governor of Buenos Aires took everything, but I still have your heart. Come to me. Your presence will either give me back life or cause me to die of happiness.

This charming, unhoped-for letter filled Candide with inexpressible joy, and the illness of his beloved Cunégonde overwhelmed him with grief. Torn between these two feelings, he took his gold and diamonds and had Martin lead him to the inn in which Mademoiselle Cunégonde was staying. He entered her room trembling with emotion, his heart pounding, his voice faltering. He drew back the bed curtains and called for light to be brought in.

"No, no, you mustn't!" the maid said. "Light will kill her!" And she quickly drew the bed curtains shut.

"My beloved Cunégonde!" Candide said, weeping. "How are you feeling? If you cannot see me, at least speak to me."

"She can't speak to you," the maid said.

From her bed the lady extended a plump hand, which Candide drenched with many tears and which he filled with diamonds, leaving a bag of gold on the armchair.

In the middle of his raptures, an officer of the law arrived with his men, followed by the abbé from Périgord.

"Are those the suspicious foreigners?" the officer asked.

He had them seized and ordered his men to drag them off to prison.

"In El Dorado," Candide said, "travelers are never treated like this."

"I am more of a Manichaean than ever," Martin said.

"But, Monsieur, where are you taking us?" Candide asked.

"To a dungeon," the officer replied.

Martin, having regained his composure, surmised that the lady claiming to be Cunégonde was a rogue, the abbé from Périgord a scoundrel who had jumped at the opportunity of taking advantage of Candide's innocence, and the officer of the law another rogue, who could be easily swayed.

Rather than submit himself to the procedures of justice,

Candide, enlightened by Martin's advice and still very impatient to see the real Cunégonde, offered the officer of the law three small diamonds, each worth about three thousand gold coins.

"Ah, Monsieur!" the officer with the ivory truncheon said. "Had you committed every imaginable crime, you would still be the most honest man in the world. Three diamonds! And each worth three thousand gold coins! Monsieur, I would rather die than have you thrown into a dungeon! All foreigners are arrested, but leave everything to me. I have a brother in Dieppe, in Normandy. I'll have you taken there. If you have a diamond for him too, I am sure he will take as good care of you as I would."

"But why do you arrest all foreigners?" Candide asked.

"It is because a beggar from the province of Atrebatum heard some stupid things that made him commit regicide," the abbé from Périgord replied. "Not like the regicide of 1610 in the month of May, but like the one in 1594 in the month of December, and like many more committed in other years and other months by other beggars who had heard stupid things."* The officer then explained what he meant.

"What monsters!" Candide exclaimed. "How can such horrors exist among a people that dance and sing? I want to flee as quickly as possible from this country, where monkeys taunt tigers! I have seen bears in my country, but it is only in El Dorado that I have seen true men! Officer, in the name of God, take me to Venice, where I must wait for Mademoiselle Cunégonde."

* The abbé is referring to religious zealots who attempted to assassinate French kings. Atrebatum was the Latin name for the province of Artois, birthplace of Robert-François Damiens, who made an unsuccessful assassination attempt on Louis XV. Jean Châtel failed in his attempt to assassinate Henry IV of France in 1594, but François Ravaillac succeeded in 1610.

"I can only take you to Lower Normandy," the officer said. He immediately removed Candide's irons, announced that he had been wrongly arrested, sent his men away, and took Candide and Martin to Dieppe, where he left them in his brother's care. A small Dutch vessel lay at anchor. The Norman, who with the aid of three more diamonds became the most obliging of men, helped Candide and his men board the vessel, which was about to set sail for Portsmouth in England. It did not lie on the way to Venice, but Candide believed he had found deliverance from Hell and intended to continue his journey to Venice at the first opportunity.

CHAPTER TWENTY-THREE

Candide and Martin head for the coast of England. What they see there

"Ah, Pangloss, Pangloss! Ah, Martin, Martin! Ah, my beloved Cunégonde! What is this world of ours?" Candide said onboard the Dutch vessel.

"It is both mad and abominable," Martin replied.

"Do you know England? Are people there as mad as they are in France?"

"Theirs is a different kind of madness," Martin said. "Do you know that these two nations are at war over a few acres of snow near Canada, and that they are spending more on this war than all of Canada is worth?* My limited expertise does not permit me to tell you precisely if more

* The French and Indian Wars fought between France and Britain from 1689 to 1763, when the Canadian territories known as New France were ceded to Britain in the Peace of Paris.

people are fit to be tied in one country than in the other. All I know is that the people we will encounter will all be very splenetic."

Conversing thus, they arrived at Portsmouth. A multitude of people had gathered on the shore, looking attentively at a rather fat man who was kneeling blindfolded on the deck of one of the vessels of the fleet. Four soldiers, lined up in front of the man, shot four bullets into his head with astonishing placidity, and the crowd, satisfied, dispersed.*

"What is this all about?" Candide exclaimed. "What devil is plying his trade everywhere?" He asked the name of the fat man who had just been ceremoniously executed.

"He was an admiral," Candide was told.

"And why was the admiral executed?"

"Because he didn't have enough people killed. He fought a battle with a French admiral, and it was decided that he had not drawn close enough to him."

"But the French admiral was just as far away from the English admiral as the English admiral was from the French one!" Candide said.

"That is beyond doubt," he was told. "But in this country it is good to kill an admiral from time to time to encourage the others."

Candide was so stunned and shocked by what he had seen and heard that he did not even want to set foot on land and bargained with the Dutch captain (not caring if he would rob him like the one in Surinam) to take him to Venice.

The captain was ready within two days. They sailed

* A reference to the execution of Admiral John Byng, who was put to death in 1757 after a sea battle off Minorca. Voltaire had attempted to prevent the execution.

along the French coast. They passed within sight of Lisbon, and Candide shuddered. They sailed through the strait and into the Mediterranean until they reached Venice.

"God be praised!" Candide said, embracing Martin. "It is here that I will see the fair Cunégonde again. I can rely on Cacambo as I can rely on myself. All is well, all is going well, all is the best it can possibly be."

Chapter Twenty-four

*About Paquette and Brother Giroflée**

As soon as he arrived in Venice, Candide went to look for Cacambo in all the inns and cafés, and among all the ladies of the night, but could not find him anywhere. Every day he sent messengers to all the ships and all the boats but found no news of Cacambo.

"I do not understand," Candide said to Martin. "I had enough time to travel from Surinam to Bordeaux, from Bordeaux to Paris, from Paris to Dieppe, from Dieppe to Portsmouth, to sail down the coasts of Portugal and Spain, to cross the whole Mediterranean, to spend a few months in Venice, and yet the fair Cunégonde has still not come! Instead of her I have met a hussy and an abbé from Périgord! Cunégonde must be dead, and nothing remains for me but to die too! Oh, I would have done better to stay in the paradise of El Dorado than to return to accursed Europe. How right you are, my dear Martin: everything is illusion and disaster!"

Candide sank into a black melancholy and did not visit

* *Pâquette* (more commonly, *pâquerette*) means "daisy," and *giroflée* "wallflower" or "carnation."

the opera *alla moda* or other diversions of Carnival. Not a single lady tempted him in the least.

"I must say, you are truly very naïve," Martin began, "to think that a mulatto valet with five or six million in his pockets will go off looking for your mistress at the ends of the earth and bring her to Venice for you. If he finds her, he will keep her for himself, and if he does not, he will take another. I advise you to forget your valet Cacambo and your mistress Cunégonde."

Martin was not consoling. Candide's melancholy grew, and Martin did not cease proving to him that there was little virtue or happiness on earth, except perhaps in El Dorado, where nobody could go.

While they argued on this important matter and waited for Cunégonde, Candide noticed a young Theatine monk on Saint Mark's Square, walking arm in arm with a girl.* The monk looked rosy, plump, and robust. He had sparkling eyes, a confident air, a superior look, and a proud gait. The young woman was very pretty and was singing. She looked at the monk adoringly and from time to time pinched his fat cheeks.

"At least you will admit that these people are happy," Candide said to Martin. "Until now in all the inhabitable world, except for El Dorado, I have come across only unfortunates. But as for this girl and her monk, I will wager that they are truly happy creatures."

"I will wager that they are not," Martin replied.

"We only have to invite them to dinner," Candide said, "and you will see whether I am right or not."

He immediately approached them, greeted them, and invited them to come to his inn to eat some macaroni,

* The Theatines were a monastic order founded in 1524 by Saint Cajetan and Pope Paul IV. A Theatine held no property, depending entirely on Providence.

Lombardy partridges, and caviar, and to drink some wine from Montepulciano, from Cyprus and Samos, and some Lacrimae Christi. The young lady blushed. The Theatine monk accepted the invitation. The young lady followed them, looking at Candide with surprise and confusion in her eyes, which were dimmed by a few tears. The moment she entered Candide's room she said to him, "Can it be that Monsieur Candide no longer recognizes Paquette?"

At these words, Candide, who until then had not looked at her carefully because he was thinking only of Cunégonde, said to her, "Alas, my poor child! Is it you who put Doctor Pangloss in the fine state I found him in?"

"Alas, Monsieur, it is I," Paquette replied. "I see that you have been told everything. I have heard about the terrible misfortunes that have befallen the whole house of Madame the baroness and the fair Cunégonde. I swear that my destiny has scarcely been less sad. I was exceedingly innocent when you knew me. A Franciscan who was my confessor seduced me quite easily. The consequences were terrible. I was forced to leave the castle shortly after His Lordship the Baron sent you away with kicks to the backside. If a famous doctor had not taken pity on me, I would have died. Out of gratitude, I was this doctor's mistress for a while. His wife, who was mad with jealousy, beat me pitilessly every day. She was a fury. The doctor was the ugliest of men, and I the unhappiest of creatures to be beaten continually for a man I did not love. You know, Monsieur, how dangerous it is for a splenetic woman to be the wife of a doctor. One day, incensed by his wife's conduct, he gave her, for a slight cold, a medicine that was so effective, she died within two hours in terrible convulsions. Madame's relatives brought criminal charges against Monsieur. He fled, and I was put in prison. My innocence would not have saved me had I not been fairly pretty. The judge freed me on the condition that he would succeed the doctor in my favors. I was soon succeeded by a rival and sent away without recompense, and forced to continue this terrible profession that you men find so pleasant, while to us women it is but an abyss of misery. I came to Venice to practice my profession here. Oh, Monsieur, if you could only imagine what it is like to be obliged to caress in utter indifference an old merchant, a lawyer, a monk, a gondolier, or an abbé; to be exposed to every insult, every snub, often to be reduced to borrow a dress only to have it raised by a disgusting man; to be robbed by one man of what one has earned from another; to be extorted by officers of the law; and to have no prospect before one but a terrible old age, a poorhouse, and a dunghill. If you could only imagine all this, you would conclude that I am one of the most unfortunate creatures in the world."

This is how Paquette opened her heart to the good Candide in the room of an inn and in the presence of Martin, who said to Candide, "As you can see, I have already won half the wager."

Brother Giroflée had remained in the dining room and was having a drink before dinner.

"But you seemed so cheerful when I saw you, so happy," Candide said to Paquette. "You were singing, you were caressing the Theatine monk with such natural lightheartedness. You seemed as happy then as you now claim to be unfortunate."

"Ah, Monsieur," Paquette replied, "that is another of the miseries of my trade. Yesterday I was robbed and beaten up by an officer, and today I have to seem in a good mood to please a monk."

Candide wanted to hear no more. He admitted that

Martin was right. They sat down to table with Paquette and the monk. The dinner was quite amusing, and by the end they were all speaking frankly.

"Father," Candide said to the monk. "It seems to me you are enjoying a destiny any man might envy. The flower of health glows on your face, your countenance bespeaks happiness, you have a pretty girl for your pleasure, and you seem very happy with your life as a Theatine monk."

"Upon my word, Monsieur," Brother Giroflée replied, "I wish that all Theatine monks were at the bottom of the sea. A hundred times I have been tempted to set the monastery on fire and go off to become a Turk. My parents forced me at the age of fifteen to don this repugnant habit so they could leave a larger fortune to my accursed older brother, may God confound him! Jealousy, discord, and anger are rampant in the monastery. It is true I have preached a few bad sermons that have earned me a little money, of which the prior steals half—the rest I use to keep girls. But when I return to the monastery in the evening, I am ready to bang my head against the walls of the dormitory. And all my brother monks are in the same predicament."

Martin turned to Candide with his usual composure. "Well," he said, "have I not won the entire wager?"

Candide gave Paquette two thousand piastres and Brother Giroflée a thousand.

"I assure you that with this they will be happy," Candide said to Martin.

"I do not believe that for a moment," Martin said. "You may well be making them much more unhappy with those piastres."

"What will be will be," Candide replied. "But one thing consoles me: I see that one often meets people that one was sure one would never see again. It may well be that since I came across my red sheep and Paquette again, I might also come across Cunégonde."

"I hope that she will make you happy one day," Martin said. "But it is something I truly doubt."

"You are a hard man," Candide replied.

"It is because I have lived," Martin said.

"But take a look at those gondoliers," Candide said. "Aren't they constantly singing?"

"You don't see them at home with their wives and gaggles of brats," Martin said. "The doge has his worries, the gondoliers have theirs. But it is true that, all in all, the lot of a gondolier is preferable to that of a doge. Yet I think the difference is so trivial that it is not worth discussing."

"I hear a lot about Senator Pococurante," Candide said, "who lives in that beautiful palazzo on the Brenta, and who receives foreigners with great hospitality.* People claim that he is a man who has never met with any sorrows."

"I would like to see this rare specimen," Martin said.

Candide immediately sent a message to Senator Pococurante requesting permission to call on him the following day.

Chapter Twenty-five

The visit to Senator Pococurante, a Venetian nobleman

Candide and Martin traveled by gondola along the Brenta and arrived at the palazzo of the nobleman Pococurante. The gardens were well maintained and adorned with beautiful marble statues. The palazzo was an exquisite piece of

* *Pococurante* in Italian means "caring little."

architecture. The master of the house, a sixty-year-old man of extreme wealth, received the two inquisitive visitors with much politeness but little enthusiasm, which disconcerted Candide but did not displease Martin at all.

First, two pretty, neatly dressed girls served cocoa that they had foamed up very nicely. Candide could not refrain from praising their beauty, grace, and adroitness.

"They are quite good creatures," Senator Pococurante said. "I sometimes have them sleep in my bed, as I am rather tired of the ladies of the town, with their coquetry, jealousy, squabbles, humors, pettiness, pride, foolishness, and the sonnets one has to compose or commission for them. And yet, these two are also beginning to bore me."

After lunch Candide, ambling through a long gallery, was surprised by the beauty of the paintings. He asked which master had painted the first two.

"They are by Raphael," the senator said. "Vanity led me to buy them quite expensively a few years ago. Word has it that they are the most beautiful paintings in Italy, but I don't like them at all. The color is too brownish, the figures are not sufficiently fleshed out or conspicuous enough, and those draperies bear no resemblance to cloth. In a word, despite what everyone says, I do not find them a true imitation of nature. I can't like a painting unless I can believe I am seeing nature itself, and there are none of that kind. I have many paintings, but I no longer look at them."

While they waited for dinner, Pococurante ordered a concerto to be performed. Candide found the music exquisite.

"This noise might amuse one for half an hour or so," Pococurante said, "but if it lasts longer it becomes tiring, even if nobody dares admit it. Music today is no more than the art of executing difficult things, and what is merely difficult cannot please one for long. I would perhaps prefer opera, had they not discovered the secret of turning it into a monster that revolts me. I do not mind if people want to see bad tragedies set to music, the scenes serving only to introduce (and quite badly) one or two ridiculous songs intended to exhibit the actress's gullet. Good luck to those who wish to swoon with pleasure or are able to do so at seeing a castrato strutting awkwardly over the stage, squawking away at the role of Caesar or Cato. As for me, I long ago turned my back on these paltry things that nowadays are the glory of Italy, and for which sovereigns pay so dearly."

Candide argued a little, but tactfully. Martin agreed completely with the senator.

They sat down at table and after an excellent dinner went into the library. Candide, seeing a magnificently bound volume of Homer, praised the illustrious senator for his good taste.

"This is a book that delighted the great Pangloss, the best philosopher in all Germany," he said.

"It doesn't delight me," Pococurante replied coldly. "I was once led to believe that I enjoyed reading it. But the constant repetition of the battles that are all alike; the gods who always choose to act without deciding anything; Helen, who is the reason for the war but scarcely plays a role; Troy, which is besieged but never taken; all this did nothing but inspire the greatest boredom in me. I have asked several scholars if they were as bored as I was when they read Homer, and all those among them who were sincere admitted that the book never failed to put them to sleep, but that it was important to exhibit it in one's library, like an ancient monument, or rusty coins that can no longer be used in commerce."

"Surely Your Excellency does not hold the same opinion of Virgil," Candide said.

"I will concede," Pococurante said, "that the second, fourth, and sixth books of his *Aeneid* are excellent. But as for his pious Aeneas, his brawny Cloanthus, his steadfast Achates, little Ascanius, the idiotic King Latinus, the common Amata, and the insipid Lavinia, I do not think you will find anything more cold or disagreeable. I prefer Tasso, or Ariosto's tales that put you to sleep."

"Might I venture to ask if Your Excellency does not take great pleasure in reading Horace?" Candide asked.

"He has some maxims from which a man of the world can profit," Pococurante replied, "and as these are squeezed into lively verse, they easily etch themselves in one's memory. But I care very little for his journey to Brindisi, or his description of a bad dinner, or that squabble between pilferers, where some fellow called Pupilus supposedly spoke words *full of pus*, while the other rogue spoke words that were *vinegar.** And I found his crude verses attacking old women and witches in bad taste, nor do I see the point of his telling his friend Maecenas that if he were placed among the ranks of lyric poets he would strike the stars with his sublime brow.† Fools will admire everything in a revered author; I read only for myself. I like only what is of use to me."

Candide, who had been brought up never to judge anything for himself, was quite astonished by what he heard, but Martin thought that Pococurante's way of thinking was quite reasonable.

* Pococurante is referring to Horace's *Satires,* I. v, II. viii, and I. vii. He mispronounces Rupilius as Pupilus, comically mistaking the character in the satire for the famous Roman consul and general Publius Rupilius.

† "His crude verses attacking old women and witches" refers to *Satires,* I. viii, and *Epodes,* particularly v, viii, xii, and xvii. Caius Cilnius Maecenas was Emperor Augustus's chief adviser and a patron of the arts. Horace dedicated the first three books of his odes to him. "Striking the stars with his sublime brow" is the last line of Ode I. i.

"Ah, I see a volume of Cicero here," said Candide. "I imagine you would never tire of reading that great man."

"I never read him," the Venetian replied. "What do I care if he pleaded for Rabirius or Cluentius?* I have enough lawsuits to judge. I might have liked his philosophical works, but when I saw that he doubts everything, I came to the conclusion that I know as much as he does, and that I do not need anyone's help to be ignorant."

"Ah, here are eighty volumes of the collected papers of a scientific academy," Martin exclaimed. "There might be something of interest in them."

"There would be," Pococurante replied, "if a single one of the authors of that hodgepodge had at least invented the art of making pins. But in all those volumes there is nothing but pointless systems, and not a single useful thing."

"How many plays I see here!" Candide said. "In Italian, Spanish, and French!"

"Yes," the senator replied. "I have three thousand of them, but there are not three dozen that are good. As for those collections of sermons, which all together are not worth a single page of Seneca, and all those fat volumes of theology, you can be certain that I never open them. Neither I nor anyone else."

Martin noticed shelves filled with English books. "I believe that a republican must for the most part enjoy these works that were written in such a liberal spirit," he said.

"Yes," Pococurante replied, "it is nice to write what one thinks. It is the privilege of man. But in all of Italy we only write what we do *not* think. Those who live in the land of the Caesars and Anthonys do not dare entertain a single idea without the permission of a Dominican. I would be

* Two speeches of Cicero, "Pro Rabirio" and "Pro Cluentio."

happy with the liberty that inspires those English geniuses, if partisan passion and spirit did not corrupt everything that is admirable in this precious liberty."

Candide, seeing a volume of Milton, asked Pococurante if he did not consider that author a great man.

"Him, a great man?" Pococurante exclaimed. "That barbarian, who wrote an endless commentary on the first chapter of Genesis in ten books of dour verse? That crude imitator of the Greeks, who mutilates creation and who, while Moses represents the Eternal Being as creating the world by the word, has the Messiah take up a grand pair of compasses from a cupboard in Heaven in order to trace his work? You expect me to esteem the man who has ruined Hell and Tasso's Devil, who disguises Lucifer sometimes as a toad and sometimes as a pygmy, who makes him keep reshuffling the same speeches a hundred times, who makes him argue theology, who takes Ariosto's comic invention of firearms seriously and has devils firing cannons in Heaven? Neither I nor anyone else in Italy can possibly take pleasure in all this distressing extravagance. The marriage of Sin and Death and the vipers that Sin engenders are enough to turn the stomach of any man of delicacy and taste, and Milton's long description of a hospital can benefit only a gravedigger. That obscure, bizarre, and disgusting poem was despised at its birth, and I treat it today as it was treated in its own country by its contemporaries! In any case, I say what I think, and care little if others think as I do."

These words distressed Candide. He respected Homer and felt some liking for Milton. "Alas," he said in a low voice to Martin, "I am afraid that this man will hold our German poets in utter contempt."

"There would be no great harm in that," Martin replied.

"Oh, what a great man," Candide whispered. "What a genius this Pococurante is. Nothing can please him!"

After having looked at all the books, they went down into the garden. Candide praised each of its beauties.

"I have never seen anything matching this garden in bad taste," Pococurante said. "We have nothing but trifles here. But starting tomorrow I will have them plant a garden of more noble design."

After the two inquisitive guests had taken leave of His Excellency, Candide said to Martin, "Well now, you must agree that he is the happiest of men, as he is superior to everything he possesses."

"Don't you see that everything he possesses disgusts him?" Martin replied. "Plato said a long time ago that the best stomachs are not the ones that reject all food."

"But isn't there pleasure in criticizing everything, in perceiving faults where other men see beauty?" Candide asked.

"Are you saying that there is pleasure in not having pleasure?" Martin replied.

"Well," Candide said, "no man can be happy, except for me when I see Cunégonde again."

"It is always good to hope," Martin said.

But the days and weeks passed. Cacambo did not return, and Candide was so sunk in grief that he did not even wonder why Paquette and Brother Giroflée had not come to thank him.

Chapter Twenty-six

Of a dinner that Candide and Martin had with six strangers, and who they were

One evening, when Candide and Martin were about to sit down at table with some strangers staying at their inn, a man whose face was the color of soot approached Candide from behind, took him by the arm, and said, "Be ready to leave with us, be ready without fail!"

Candide turned and saw Cacambo. Only the sight of Cunégonde could have surprised and pleased him more. He was almost crazed with joy. He embraced his dear friend. "Cunégonde must be here, I am certain of it! Where is she? Take me to her so I may die of happiness with her."

"Cunégonde is not here," Cacambo replied. "She is in Constantinople."

"Heavens! In Constantinople? But even if she were in China, I would fly to her! Let us leave right away!"

"We shall leave after dinner," Cacambo replied. "I cannot tell you more. I am a slave, and my master is waiting for me. I must go and serve him at table. Do not say a word. Dine, and be ready to depart."

Candide was torn between joy and grief, delighted at seeing his faithful emissary again and astonished to see him a slave. He was filled with the idea of finding his mistress once more, his heart agitated, his mind in turmoil. He sat at table with Martin, who regarded all these adventures with cool composure, and with six foreigners who had come to spend the Carnival in Venice.

Cacambo, who was pouring wine for one of the foreigners, leaned down to his ear as the meal was drawing to a close and said to him, "Sire, Your Majesty may leave at will, the ship is ready."

Having spoken these words, he left. The guests were astonished and were looking at one another without uttering a word when another servant approached his master and said, "Sire, Your Majesty's carriage is in Padua, and the boat is ready." His master made a sign and the servant left. All the guests again looked at one another with redoubled surprise. A third valet approached a third foreigner and said, "Sire, Your Majesty must not remain here any longer. I shall see that all is prepared." And he, too, left.

Candide and Martin were now certain that this had to be some Carnival masquerade.

A fourth servant said to the fourth foreigner, "Your Majesty can depart at will," and left like the others. The fifth valet said the same to the fifth foreigner. But the sixth valet spoke differently to his master, who was sitting next to Candide. "On my word, Sire," he said, "no one will grant Your Majesty or me any more credit. We might both well be thrown in prison this very night. Farewell, I am going to seek my fortune elsewhere."

All the servants had disappeared, and Candide, Martin, and the six strangers sat in profound silence, which Candide finally broke. "Gentlemen," he said. "This is a peculiar joke indeed. How can it be that you all are kings? As for me, I can vouch that neither I nor Martin is a king."

Cacambo's master replied gravely in Italian: "I am not joking. I am Ahmed III. I was Grand Sultan for some years. I dethroned my brother and was dethroned by my nephew. My viziers' throats were cut. I am spending my life in the old seraglio. My nephew, Grand Sultan Mahmud, sometimes allows me to travel for my health, and I have come to spend the Carnival in Venice." *

A young man seated next to Ahmed spoke after him: "My name is Ivan. I was Emperor of all the Russias. I was dethroned in my cradle, my mother and father imprisoned.† I was raised in prison. I am sometimes granted permission to travel, accompanied by those who guard me, and I have come to spend the Carnival in Venice."

The third said: "I am Charles Edward, King of England. My father yielded me the rights to his kingdom.‡ I fought to keep them. The hearts of eight thousand of my partisans were ripped out and thrown in their faces.§ I was imprisoned. I am going to Rome to visit my father the king, who was dethroned as I and my grandfather were, and I have come to spend the Carnival in Venice."

The fourth now spoke: "I am the King of the Poles. The fortunes of war have deprived me of my hereditary states. My father suffered the same misfortune.** I resign myself to Providence, as Sultan Ahmed, Emperor Ivan, and King Charles Edward—to whom God may grant a long life—have done, and I have come to spend the Carnival in Venice."

* Ahmed III, 1637–1736, became Sultan of the Ottoman Empire in 1703, when his brother Mustafa II abdicated. In 1730, Ahmed III abdicated in favor of his nephew Mahmud I.

† Ivan VI, 1740–1764, was known as the Infant Emperor, nominally reigning from 1740 to 1741. He grew up in solitary confinement in various prisons.

‡ Charles Edward Stuart, 1720–1788, also known as "The Young Pretender" and "Bonnie Prince Charlie," was the grandson of the deposed King James II of England and the son of James Stuart, "The Old Pretender," who had tried to invade Scotland twice in the hope of seizing the British throne.

§ A reference to the Battle of Culloden Moor, 1746.

** Augustus III, 1696–1763, King of Poland, was dethroned by Frederick the Great. His father, Augustus II, had been dethroned in 1704 by Charles XII of Sweden, who placed Stanislaw I on the throne.

The fifth said: "I am also the King of the Poles. I have lost my kingdom twice, but Providence gave me another state in which I have done more good than all the Sarmatian kings together were ever able to do on the banks of the Vistula.* I also resign myself to Providence, and I have come to spend the Carnival in Venice."

It remained for the sixth monarch to speak. "Gentlemen," he said. "I am not as grand a king as you, but I was as much a king as any other. I am Theodor. I was elected King of Corsica.† People addressed me as 'Your Majesty,' though now they barely call me 'Monsieur.' I had coins minted, and now I do not have a single one left. I had two secretaries of state, now I barely have a valet. I saw myself on a throne and spent a long time lying on straw in a London prison. I am afraid that I might well be treated the same way here, even though I have come, like Your Majesties, to spend the Carnival in Venice."

The five other kings listened to his speech with noble compassion. Each gave twenty gold coins to King Theodor so that he could buy clothes and linen. Candide made him a present of a diamond worth two thousand gold coins. "Who is this private citizen, who is able to give a hundred times more than each of us can, and gives it?" the five kings wondered.

* Stanislaw Leszczynski, 1677–1766, was King Stanislas I of Poland from 1704 to 1709, and from 1733 to 1735. He lost the throne to his other Polish table companion, Augustus III.

"Providence gave me another state": Leszcynski became Duc de Lorraine and had considerable influence in France, as his daughter, Maria, married Louis XV. The ancient Sarmatian Empire covered Poland and much of Russia.

† The Westphalian baron Theodor von Neuhof, 1694–1756, was a gambler and adventurer who managed to rouse the Corsicans into electing him their king. He ruled Corsica as King Theodor I from April to November 1736. In 1749 he was imprisoned in London for his debts.

As they rose from table, four more serene highnesses who had lost their states through the fortunes of war arrived at the inn to spend the rest of the Carnival in Venice. But Candide paid no attention to these new arrivals. His only thought was to set out and find his beloved Cunégonde in Constantinople.

Chapter Twenty-seven

Candide's voyage to Constantinople

The faithful Cacambo had already arranged with the Turkish captain, who was taking Sultan Ahmed back to Constantinople, to take Candide and Martin onboard. Both embarked after prostrating themselves before His miserable Highness. Along the way, Candide had said to Martin, "We dined with six dethroned kings, and even among these six kings there was one to whom I gave alms. Perhaps there are many more princes who are even more unfortunate. For my part, I have only lost a hundred sheep and am going to fly into Cunégonde's arms. My dear Martin, I must say once again that Pangloss was right: All is for the best."

"I hope so," Martin replied.

"But that was quite an improbable adventure we had in Venice," Candide said. "No one has ever seen or heard tell of six dethroned kings dining together at an inn."

"It is not any more extraordinary than most of the things that have happened to us," Martin replied. "It is very common for kings to be dethroned. And as for the honor we were accorded of dining with them, it is a trifle not even worth our attention."

Scarcely had Candide set foot on the ship when he

threw his arms around his former valet, his friend Cacambo.

"Well," he asked, "what is Cunégonde doing? Is she still a paragon of beauty? Does she still love me? Is she well? No doubt you bought her a palace in Constantinople."

"My dear master," Cacambo replied. "Cunégonde is washing dishes on the shores of the Propontis for a prince who has very few dishes. She is a slave in the house of a former sovereign named Rákóczi to whom the Grand Turk gives three crowns a day in his exile.* But what is even more sad is that she has lost her beauty and become horribly ugly."

"Well, whether she is beautiful or ugly now," Candide replied, "I am an honest man, and it is my duty to love her forever. But how could she have been reduced to such an abject state with the five or six million that you had with you?"

"Well," Cacambo replied, "did I not have to give two million to Don Fernando d'Ibarra y Figueroa y Mascarenes y Lampourdos y Souza, the Governor of Buenos Aires, to secure his permission to retrieve Mademoiselle Cunégonde? And didn't a pirate graciously strip us of all the rest? And didn't that pirate take us to Cape Mapatan, Milos, Icaria, Samos, Petra, the Dardanelles, Marmara, and Scutari? Cunégonde and the old woman are in the service of the prince I mentioned, and I am the slave of the dethroned sultan."

"What a terrible string of calamities!" Candide said.

* Francis II (Ferenc Rákóczi), 1676–1735, Transylvanian prince and a national hero of Hungary, was elected "ruling prince" of Hungary in 1704 after leading a successful rebellion against the Habsburgs. In 1711, after the Habsburgs regained control of Hungary, Rákóczi fled into exile, finally settling in the Ottoman Empire, in Tekirdag on the Sea of Marmara.

"But I still have a few diamonds and will be able to free Cunégonde easily enough. It is a pity, though, that she has become so ugly." Then, turning to Martin, he said, "Who do you think is to be pitied most, Emperor Ahmed, Emperor Ivan, King Charles Edward, or I?"

"That I do not know," Martin replied. "I would need to be able to look into all your hearts to answer that."

"Ah," said Candide, "were Pangloss here, he would know and would instruct us."

"I do not know with what scales your Doctor Pangloss would have been able to weigh the misfortunes of men and estimate their pains," said Martin. "All I can presume is that there are millions of men on earth who are a hundred times more worthy of pity than King Charles Edward, Emperor Ivan, or Sultan Ahmed."

"That may well be," Candide replied.

Within a few days they arrived at the straits of the Black Sea. First Candide bought back Cacambo at a very high price, and without losing any time, he and his companions boarded a galley in order to set out for the shore of the Propontis to search for Cunégonde, no matter how ugly she might be.

Among the galley convicts were two who rowed very badly and whose bare shoulders the Levantine captain lashed from time to time with a bullwhip. Candide's nature inclined him to look at them more carefully than the other convicts, and he approached them with pity. Some of the features in their disfigured faces seemed to resemble those of Pangloss and of the unfortunate Jesuit baron, Cunégonde's brother. This impression moved and saddened Candide. He looked at them even more carefully.

"In truth," he said to Cacambo, "had I not seen Doctor Pangloss hanged and had I not had the misfortune of killing the baron myself, I would think it is they who are rowing in this galley!"

At the words *baron* and *Pangloss,* the two convicts uttered a great cry, sat stock-still on their bench, and dropped their oars. The Levantine captain rushed at them, redoubling the lashes of his whip.

"Stop, stop, Captain!" Candide cried. "I shall give you as much money as you want!"

"What? It is Candide!" one of the convicts said.

"What? It is Candide!" the other convict said.

"Is this a dream?" Candide exclaimed. "Am I awake? Am I on this galley? Is this His Lordship the Baron, whom I killed? Is this Doctor Pangloss, whom I saw hanged?"

"It is us, it is us!" they replied.

"What? This is the great philosopher?" Martin asked.

"Hey, Levantine Captain!" Candide said. "How much ransom do you want for Monsieur Thunder-Ten-Tronckh, one of the foremost barons of the Empire, and Monsieur Pangloss, Germany's most profound metaphysician?"

"Christian dog," the Levantine captain replied. "As these Christian galley-slave dogs are barons and metaphysicians, which doubtless is a great dignity in their country, you must give me fifty thousand gold coins."

"You shall have them, Monsieur. Take me with the speed of lightning to Constantinople, and you will be paid immediately. But wait! On second thought, take me straight to Mademoiselle Cunégonde."

No sooner had Candide made the offer than the Levantine captain pointed his prow toward the city and made the convicts row faster than a bird cleaves the air.

Candide embraced the baron and Pangloss a hundred times.

"How can it be that I did not kill you, my dear Baron?

And my dear Pangloss, how can it be that you are alive after being hanged? And why are both of you on a galley in Turkey?"

"Is it true that my beloved sister is in this country?" the baron asked.

"Yes," Cacambo replied.

"So I see my dear Candide again!" Pangloss exclaimed.

Candide introduced Martin and Cacambo. They all embraced and all spoke at the same time. The galley was flying—they had already arrived in the port. A Jew was summoned to whom Candide sold a diamond worth a hundred thousand gold coins for fifty thousand and who swore by Abraham that he could not give him more. Candide immediately paid the ransom for the baron and Pangloss. The latter threw himself at the feet of his liberator and bathed them in tears. The baron thanked him with a nod and promised to return the money at the first opportunity.

"But is it possible that my sister is in Turkey?" he said.

"Nothing is more possible," Cacambo said, "as she is washing dishes for a Transylvanian prince."

Two Jews were immediately summoned. Candide sold some more diamonds, and they all set out in another galley to rescue Cunégonde.

Chapter Twenty-eight

What happened to Candide, Cunégonde, Pangloss, Martin, et cetera

"I beg you once again to forgive me, Reverend Father, for having driven my sword through you," Candide said to the baron.

"Let us speak no more of it," the baron replied. "I admit

I was a little too rash myself. But as you wish to know the circumstances that brought me to the galleys, I will tell you: After the brother apothecary of the collegium healed my wound, I was attacked by a Spanish detachment and abducted. I was imprisoned in Buenos Aires just after my sister had left. I asked to be allowed to return to the Father General in Rome. There, I was appointed to serve as almoner to the French ambassador in Constantinople. I had not been at my post for a week when one evening I came across a very handsome young page from the sultan's palace. It was very hot, and the young man wanted to bathe. I seized the opportunity to bathe too. I did not know that it was a capital offense for a Christian to be found naked with a young Moslem. A cadi ordered that I be dealt a hundred strokes with a stick on the soles of my feet and sentenced to the galleys.* I do not think that a more horrible injustice could have been committed. But I would like to know why my sister is in the kitchen of a sovereign of Transylvania who has taken refuge among the Turks."

"But you, my dear Pangloss," Candide said. "How can it be that I see you again?"

"It is true that you saw me being hanged," Pangloss replied. "According to custom I ought to have been burned, but if you remember, there had been a downpour just as they were preparing to cook me. The storm was so violent that they despaired of lighting the fire. I was hanged, as that was the best they could do. A surgeon purchased my body, took me to his house, and dissected me. First he made a cross-shaped incision from my navel to my clavicle. One could not have been hanged more poorly than I had been. The Executor of the High Offices of the Holy Inquisition,

* A cadi was a civil judge in Turkey.

who was a subdeacon, was a wonderful expert at burning people but was not accustomed to hanging. My rope was wet. It did not slide properly and became knotted. In short, I was still breathing.

The cross-shaped incision made me utter such a loud cry that the surgeon fell over, and thinking that he was dissecting the Devil, he ran away in mortal terror, falling down the stairs as he fled. With all the noise, his wife came running and saw me lying on the table with my cross-shaped incision. She was even more terrified than her husband, fled, and tumbled over him. When they had recovered a little, I heard her say to her husband, 'My dear, what could possibly have induced you to dissect a heretic? Don't you know that the Devil is always inside those people's bodies? I'll quickly look for a priest to exorcise him.' I shuddered at these words, gathered the little strength I still had left, and shouted, 'Have pity on me!' Finally the Portuguese barber took courage and sewed me up again.* His wife even tended me. I was back on my feet in two weeks. The barber secured me a position as lackey to a Knight of Malta who was going to Venice, but as my master could not pay me, I went into the service of a Venetian merchant and followed him to Constantinople.

"One day, it took my fancy to enter a mosque. There was only an old imam there with a very pretty young worshiper saying her paternosters. Her bosom was completely uncovered, and between her breasts there was a beautiful bouquet of tulips, roses, anemones, buttercups, hyacinths, and auriculas. She dropped her bouquet. I picked it up and put it back with respectful attentiveness. It took me so long that the imam became angry and, seeing that I was a Chris-

* Pangloss is referring to the surgeon as a barber, as during the eighteenth century surgeons were still barbers by profession.

tian, called for help. I was taken to the cadi, who ordered that I be dealt a hundred strokes of a stick on the soles of my feet and sent to the galleys. I was chained in the same galley and on the same bench as His Lordship the Baron. In this galley were four young men from Marseilles, five Neapolitan priests, and two monks from Corfu, who told us that such adventures occurred every day. His Lordship the Baron claimed that he had suffered a greater injustice than I had. For my part, I claimed that it was far more permissible to replace a bouquet between a woman's breasts than to be completely naked with a page. We argued ceaselessly and were receiving twenty lashes of the bullwhip every day when the chain of events in this universe led you to our galley and you ransomed us."

"Well, my dear Pangloss," Candide said. "After you were hanged, dissected, beaten black and blue, and had to row in the galleys, did you continue to believe that everything is for the best in the world?"

"I am still of my former opinion," Pangloss replied, "for I am a philosopher, after all, and it would be improper for me to recant, as Leibniz cannot be wrong. Preestablished harmony is the most beautiful thing in the world, as are the plenum and subtle matter."*

* *Plenum* denotes the conception of space as entirely filled with matter. Leibniz wrote in *Monadology* (1714), entry 61, "As all is a plenum, all matter is connected."

Chapter Twenty-nine

How Candide found Cunégonde and the old woman

While Candide, the baron, Pangloss, Martin, and Cacambo recounted their adventures, debating on the contingent and noncontingent events of this universe, arguing about effects and causes, about physical evil and moral evil, freedom and necessity, and the consolations one can find on a Turkish galley, they arrived at the house of the Prince of Transylvania on the shore of Propontis. The first two things they saw were Cunégonde and the old woman, who were hanging towels on a line to dry.

The baron paled at the sight. Candide, the tender lover, seeing his beautiful Cunégonde browned and dried by the sun, her eyes bloodshot, her breasts withered, her cheeks wrinkled, her hands red and scaly, recoiled three paces in horror, but good manners made him step forward. She embraced Candide and her brother. They embraced the old woman. Candide bought both their freedom.

There was a small farm nearby, which the old woman suggested Candide should occupy while they all waited for a better destiny. As nobody had told her, Cunégonde was not aware that she had grown ugly, and she reminded Candide of his promises in such a peremptory tone that he did not dare refuse her. So he went to tell the baron that he was going to marry his sister.

"I will not stand for such baseness on her part, or such insolence on yours!" the baron said. "I will never be reproached with having consented to such infamy. My sister's children could never enter the ranks of the German nobility. No! My sister shall never marry anyone but a baron of the Empire!"

Cunégonde threw herself at her brother's feet and bathed them with tears. He remained inflexible.

"You fool of a baron!" Candide exclaimed. "I freed you from the galleys, paid your ransom, and paid your sister's ransom. She was washing dishes here, she is ugly, I have the goodness of heart to make her my wife, and still you oppose the marriage? If I were to trust my anger, I would kill you again."

"You can kill me again," the baron said, "but you shall not marry my sister while I am alive."

Chapter Thirty

Conclusion

At the bottom of his heart, Candide had no wish to marry Cunégonde, but the baron's insolence made him determined to go forward with the marriage, and Cunégonde urged him so energetically that he felt he could not go back on his word. He consulted Pangloss, Martin, and faithful Cacambo. Pangloss delivered a fine dissertation by which he proved that the baron had no rights whatsoever over his sister, and that the laws of the Empire allowed for her to enter into a morganatic marriage with Candide. Martin declared that they should throw the baron into the sea. Cacambo suggested that they return the baron to the Levantine captain and the galleys, after which he would be sent to the Father General in Rome on the first available ship. This idea was thought very good indeed. The old woman approved. Cunégonde was not told anything. The matter was settled with the payment of a small sum of money, and they had the double pleasure of trapping a Jesuit and punishing a German baron.

It would be quite natural to imagine that after so many disasters Candide would live the most pleasant life in the world: He was finally married to his mistress and living with the philosopher Pangloss, the philosopher Martin, wise Cacambo, and the old woman, and he had brought back many diamonds from the land of the ancient Incas. But he was tricked and swindled by the Jews until he had nothing left but the little farm. His wife became uglier every day and grew shrewish and unbearable. The old woman was ailing and in an even worse mood than Cunégonde. Cacambo, who tended the garden and went to Constantinople to sell vegetables, was worn out by the hard work and cursed his fate. Pangloss was distraught at not shining at a university in Germany. As for Martin, he was determinedly convinced that one is badly off wherever one might be. He bore everything patiently.

Candide, Martin, and Pangloss sometimes debated metaphysics and morals. They often saw boats passing beneath the windows of the farm, carrying effendis, pashas, and cadis being sent to exile in Lemnos, Mytilene, and Erzurum. They saw other cadis, pashas, and effendis coming to take the place of those who had been expelled, and who then were expelled in their turn. They saw exquisitely stuffed heads that were on their way to be presented to the sultan. These spectacles redoubled their debates. And when they were not disputing, their boredom was so excessive that the old woman one day went so far as to say, "I would like to know what is worse: being violated a hundred times by Negro pirates, having a buttock cut off, running the gauntlet in the Bulgar army, being whipped and hanged in an auto-da-fé, being dissected, rowing in a galley, suffering all the miseries we have been through, or simply sitting around here without doing anything?"

"That is a difficult question," Candide replied.

Her words gave rise to new deliberations, and Martin concluded that man is born to live either in convulsions of apprehension or the lethargy of boredom. Candide did not agree but expressed no opinion. Pangloss declared that he had always suffered horribly, but having asserted that everything was going wonderfully, he would continue to assert it, even though he did not believe it in the least.

There was one event that served to confirm Martin in his detestable principles, to make Candide hesitate more than ever, and put Pangloss in a predicament. It was the arrival at the farm one day of Paquette and Brother Giroflée, who had fallen into the most wretched poverty. They had quickly run through their three thousand piastres, left each other, made up again, quarreled, been thrown in prison, escaped, and finally Brother Giroflée had gone off to become a Turk. Paquette continued practicing her trade everywhere but was no longer earning anything.

"I had foreseen that your gift to them would soon be squandered and would only make them more wretched than before," Martin told Candide. "You were rolling in millions of piastres, you and Cacambo, and you are not much happier than Brother Giroflée and Paquette."

"Ah, so the heavens have brought you back to us, my poor child, " Pangloss said to Paquette. "Are you aware that you cost me the tip of my nose, an eye, and an ear? And look at you now! Oh, what a world we live in!"

This new event led them to philosophize more than ever.

There was a famous dervish in the neighborhood who was thought to be the best philosopher in all of Turkey. They went to consult him.

"Master," Pangloss said, "we have come to beg you to tell us why an animal as strange as man was created."

"Why are you sticking your nose into such things?" the dervish replied. "Is it any of your business?"

"But Reverend Father," Candide said to him, "there is a horrible amount of evil in the world."

"What does it matter whether there is good or evil," the dervish replied. "When His Highness the Sultan sends a vessel to Egypt, does His Highness concern himself whether the mice onboard are snugly settled or not?"

"So what should we do?" Pangloss asked.

"You should keep quiet," the dervish replied.

"I had flattered myself that I might be able to debate with you a little about effects and causes of the best of all possible worlds, the origin of evil, the nature of the soul, and preestablished harmony," Pangloss said.

On hearing these words the dervish slammed the door in their faces.

During this exchange, news had spread that two viziers of the sultan and the mufti had been strangled in Constantinople and that a number of their friends had been impaled.* This catastrophe caused great commotion for several hours. Pangloss, Candide, and Martin, returning to their small farm, came across a good old man who was enjoying the cool shade under a grove of orange trees before his door. Pangloss, who was as prone to curiosity as he was to reasoning, asked him the name of the mufti who had been strangled.

"I have no idea," the gentleman replied. "I have never known the name of any mufti or vizier. I know absolutely nothing of the incident you are telling me about. I presume that in general those who are involved in public affairs sometimes die miserably, and deservedly so. But I never inform

* In the Ottoman Empire, the mufti was the official head of the Islamic state religion.

myself of what is going on in Constantinople. I am contented simply to send the fruits of the garden I cultivate to be sold there."

Having spoken these words, he asked the strangers into his house. His two daughters and two sons offered them a number of different sherbets they had made themselves, some sweet cream flavored with candied citron rind, oranges, lemons, limes, pineapples, and pistachios, as well as mocha coffee that was not mixed with bad coffee from Batavia or the East Indies. Afterward, the two daughters of the good Moslem perfumed the beards of Candide, Pangloss, and Martin.

"You must have a vast and magnificent estate," Candide said to the Turk.

"I only have about twenty-five acres," the Turk replied. "I cultivate it with my children. Work keeps three great evils at bay: boredom, vice, and want."

Returning to his farm, Candide profoundly reflected on what the Turk had said. "That fine old man seems to have secured himself a better fate than that of the six kings with whom we had the honor to dine," he said to Pangloss and Martin.

"Greatness, all the philosophers agree, is fraught with peril," Pangloss replied. "After all, Eglon, King of the Moabites, was assassinated by Ehud; Absalom was hung by his hair and run through by three spears; King Nadab, son of Jeroboam, was killed by Baasha, King Elah by Zimri, Ahaziah by Jehu, Athaliah by Jehoiada, and the Kings Jehoiakim, Jeconiah, and Zedekiah were enslaved. And do you know the end of Croesus, Astyages, Darius, Dionysius of Syracuse, Pyrrhus, Perseus, Hannibal, Jugurtha, Ariovistus, Caesar, Pompey, Nero, Otho, Vitellius, Domitian, Richard II of England, Edward II, Henry VI, Richard III,

Mary Stuart, Charles I, the three Henrys of France, and the emperor Henry IV? Do you know—"

"I also know," Candide said, "that we must cultivate our garden."

"You are right," Pangloss replied, "for when man was placed in the Garden of Eden, he was placed there *ut operaretur eum*—'in order to cultivate it.'* Which proves that man was not born for leisure.

"Let us work without reasoning," Martin said. "It is the only way to make life bearable."

Everyone in the little group entered into this commendable scheme, each resolved to exercise his talents. The small estate yielded plentifully. Cunégonde was, in truth, exceptionally ugly, but she did become an excellent baker. Paquette embroidered, and the old woman saw to the laundry. Everyone, even Brother Giroflée, did something useful: he was a very good carpenter, and even became an honest man. And Pangloss sometimes said to Candide, "All events are linked in the best of all possible worlds. After all, had you not been chased from a fine castle with hard kicks to your backside for love of Mademoiselle Cunégonde, had you not been brought before the Inquisition, had not walked the length and breadth of the Americas on foot, not run your sword through the baron, not lost all your sheep of the fine land of El Dorado, you would not be eating candied citrons and pistachios."

"That is well said," Candide replied, "but we must cultivate our garden."

* An altered quotation from Gen. 2:15 in the Vulgate: "Tulit ergo Dominus Deus hominem et posuit eum in paradiso voluptatis ut operatur et custodiret illum" (Then the Lord God took man and put him in the Garden of Eden to cultivate and keep it).

About the Translator

Peter Constantine was awarded the 1998 PEN Translation Prize for *Six Early Stories* by Thomas Mann, and the 1999 National Translation Award for *The Undiscovered Chekhov.* Widely acclaimed for his recent translation of the complete works of Isaac Babel, he also translated Gogol's *Taras Bulba* and *The Cossacks* by Leo Tolstoy for the Modern Library. His translations of fiction and poetry have appeared in many publications, including *The New Yorker, Harper's,* and *The Paris Review.* He lives in New York City.

A Note on the Type

The principal text of this Modern Library edition was set in a digitized version of Janson, a typeface that dates from about 1690 and was cut by Nicholas Kis, a Hungarian working in Amsterdam. The original matrices have survived and are held by the Stempel foundry in Germany. Hermann Zapf redesigned some of the weights and sizes for Stempel, basing his revisions on the original design.